Eye on the ball

By Anthony Potts

Author of *Star on the Rise* (Book 2)

Published by New Generation Publishing in 2020

ISBN

Paperback	978-1-80031-551-8
Hardback	978-1-80031-550-1
Ebook	978-1-80031-549-5

www.newgeneration-publishing.com

 New Generation Publishing

Chapter One

Mighty oaks from acorns grow...

Len gingerly stepped down from the number 122 bus, nodding his thanks to the conductor and looking and feeling every one of his 72 years. The conductor rang the bell and the bus pulled away, leaving Len standing on the edge of Clifton Marshes. He carefully lowered himself onto the bus stop bench and exchanged his well-polished brogue shoes for a pair of Wellington boots, which he had been carrying in a Woolworth's plastic bag. Len was old school, and always wore a suit, like many of his generation did. His grey hair, hidden underneath his tweed flat cap, was slicked back with Brylcreem and his suit was perfectly pressed. It was covered by a ragged, knee-length sheepskin coat, which, much like Len, had seen better days. He had learned that the marshes were no place for keeping up appearances. Before standing, he rolled up his suit trouser legs and tucked them into the sides of his boots to ensure they would also remain reasonably untouched, then he started to make his way to Pitch 24. Although still referred to as Clifton Marshes, it was basically a vast barren stretch of mud and, to a lesser extent, grass on which nearly 30 football pitches had been laid out. It was a cold October morning and the dew glistened on what grass there was. The pitches covered almost every inch of ground, with barely enough room to stand on the side without encroaching onto the pitch alongside. Goals backed onto goals, and some pitches took on peculiar dimensions due to obstacles like trees and pathways. One such pitch actually had a curve in one touchline due to a protected old oak tree that insisted on getting in the way! But despite the amateur surroundings, there was a comical air of seriousness that greeted Len as he started to make his way towards Pitch 24.

As he made his way across the field, he couldn't help but closely inspect the matches being played on either side of him - just in case.

It was clearly half-time on the first pitch he encountered – the players were all lying and sitting on the floor, sucking on the half-time orange quarters. The over-enthusiastic and rather aggressive team captain was giving the half-time team talk. "You lot just ain't taking this seriously. They're all over us, and 'alf of you look like you ain't even tryin'!" he barked between draws on his cigarette.

Len turned the fur collar of his coat up around his neck to protect himself from the wind that swept across the flat open ground. Slowly, he started to make his way further across the field, trying to avoid the muddier parts.

On the next pitch along, he was further amused at a game that had more in common with tennis than football. The few supporters resembled a Wimbledon tennis crowd watching an ongoing rally - left, right, left, right, as each team seemed incapable of retaining possession until finally it disappeared off onto another pitch.

Before long he reached Pitch 24, where Fleetdown versus Villa was about to kick off. The referee prepared to blow his whistle, and Len went and stood next to a handful of people watching. Over his many years of doing this, Len had learned that the best way to get inside information was to position himself close to the spectators. That way, he could pick up a few snippets of information about the character of those he had come to watch. He would often hear boozy anecdotes about the previous night that would leave Len doubting the suitability of the player he had come to watch. There had even been one occasion when he had heard that his target had spent the previous night in the cells due to a particularly raucous night out - Len hadn't even bothered staying to watch the game on that occasion! There had, of course, been a time when Len had not been able to go unnoticed. Every wannabe footballer had recognised Len the minute he turned up, black book in hand, wearing

2

his trademark sheepskin coat. He had to admit he missed those days, but people in football have short memories. Martin Richards, Barry Sturgess and Alex Kempster - amongst others - were now just footnotes in Clifton Rangers' history.

It was almost ten years ago that Len had discovered the last player worth writing in his black book – Alex Kempster. Alex Kempster had Len turning page after page as he mesmerised the opposition with his tricks and skills. And it had been here on this very pitch that Len had seen Martin Richards. That was back in '72 – an unusually hot September, Len remembered. He hadn't needed his sheepskin coat that day – and he hadn't needed his black book either. He was so engrossed, watching the most natural talent he had ever seen, he hadn't been able to look away to write in case he missed another special moment.

But, Len mused, his thoughts returning to the present, perhaps his sort of player was not in fashion anymore. Now it was all strength, speed and power. Len was still an optimist though, and every time he went to watch a player he held onto his belief that he might find one more "natural" to help turn around the fortunes of his beloved Rangers.

"A goal machine" was how this latest tip had been described to Len over a pint of Guinness - or two - in the Royal Oak the previous night. That goal machine had led Len to where he stood right now.

"Excuse me, would you mind telling me which one is Nigel Waters?" he said to one of the spectators.

"That's him," said the supporter, a rather rotund, thickly bearded man. Len noticed on closer inspection that this was not a spectator but a substitute player squeezed tightly into an ill-fitting shirt, "and what a bleeding player."

Len followed the man's chubby digit towards a player just taking the kick-off. The first thing that Len noticed was the boy's size: despite being only sixteen, the boy was muscular and already over six feet tall - a huge tick in the current climate. What made him look even bigger was the fact that he was standing next to a rather small, stocky lad. The smaller lad was topped with a curly mop of blonde hair that looked as out of place as he did, and his left knee was crudely wrapped in a stained tobacco-brown strapping that looked like it had seen better days.

Presently the game kicked off, and it soon became obvious that the Fleetdown players saw Nigel as their main man, and whenever they had possession, they pumped the ball in the goal machine's general direction. After a little more than ten minutes' play, Len couldn't help but notice that the small stocky lad alongside Nigel was becoming more and more uptight and frustrated. He hadn't even touched the ball yet, and Len had almost begun to feel sorry for him. On a couple of occasions he had found himself almost willing the ball towards the boy.

The game went on, and, despite a few occasions where the ball had almost bounced and bobbled into his path, Nigel hadn't looked a threat at all. Then the Fleetdown right-back, who from the evidence up to that point would have been better suited to a pastime that did not require much of a connection between brain and feet, received the ball. Once again, the intended target appeared to be Nigel. He didn't connect properly and the ball went towards the midriff of the smaller, stockier forward, who was standing unmarked inside the centre circle. It looked like the ball was going to hit him in a rather unfortunate area, but the Villa defence moved towards him to close him down anyway. Annoyed at another thwarted attack, Nigel stood still and threw his hands up in the air in irritation at the poorly delivered pass. Len, meanwhile, looked on with waning interest. All these things happened simultaneously - as did the stocky kid's reaction. As he swivelled his body, as if trying to avoid getting hit by the ball, the ball glanced off his side, somewhere around his hip, before spinning through the tiniest of gaps past the stranded defenders and in front of Nigel. With the whole defence wrong-footed, Nigel found himself clean through on goal and bearing down on the terrified keeper. Without breaking stride or glancing in the keeper's direction, Nigel blasted the ball at the goal. It just caught the underside of the bar then bounced into the net in spectacular fashion.

"Bloody brilliant!" exclaimed the overweight, bearded substitute in Len's direction, jumping up and down with more energy than you would have expected from first appearances.

Len only nodded in agreement. But his hand was a scribbling blur as he made a note in his famous black book, while remarking, more to himself than anyone else, "You might just be right…"

It was over an hour into the game, not long after Nigel's fourth goal, that Len began to make his short journey home. Turning over his third completed page of notes, he asked his bearded companion one more question then started to make his way back past the other pitches, barely glancing to either side. If you had seen him, you might have noticed a certain swagger in his step that had previously been missing; his face did not seem quite as worn either. In fact, you would have been forgiven for thinking him to be a great deal younger than his 72 years.

He arrived back to the bus stop, hoping that Harry Welch would be at home. He had a very important phone call to make…

Chapter Two

More and more often, Harry had found himself thinking back over the illustrious history of Clifton Rovers. The past seemed to sit like an anvil on his shoulders. As he looked out over the ground, Harry's thoughts wandered to the first time he had ever visited Clifton Park.

It was Bill's idea; he just wouldn't let it go. He'd rung so many times that Angela, Harry's wife, now spoke to him like a friend – she would often have a little chat before passing the phone over! With hindsight, it was obvious that Bill was going to miss out on signing Harry. He had received a few offers from clubs in Division 1 - what is now the Premier League - and that was where the real money was. In fact, Harry had been tapped up by one of the biggest clubs in the country, Tottenford, the previous season's champions. They had offered Harry a small fortune, with bonuses for everything from points to goals. Admittedly, they were looking at him as a squad member rather than starting every week, but he would be set up for life. In his head he had already signed for them.

But he hadn't discounted Clifton lightly. Both Clifton and Bill Jameson had been making waves in the footballing world. In just three years Bill Jameson had taken Clifton from Division 3 strugglers to a mid-table Division 2 team. Add to that a supportive chairman putting money into both the team and facilities and they really were a club on the rise. But like all young players, Harry wanted success, money, fame – and he wanted it *now*. The lure of the First Division was proving too strong. Nonetheless Bill was proving very persuasive, and he was certainly persistent! Finally, Harry relented and agreed to watch a game at Clifton Park. Then, after the game, meet him and let him lay out his vision!

Harry was still relatively unknown to the average fan - this was before Sky TV. For that reason, Bill had said he should mingle with the crowd and experience for himself what Bill had been talking about. It was to be a day that would change his life.

"Give me a call when you want picking up, honey," said Angela as Harry got out of the car. She then pulled away from the kerb and out into the traffic, off to bingo with her friends. Harry was left at the kerb side, unsure about what to do with the hour and a half still left before kick-off.

He looked up and down Clifton High Street, and his eyes settled on a decent-looking pub, The Royal Oak. It was his day off after all, he reasoned!

The Royal Oak was an old-fashioned English pub, with a whitewashed front, hanging baskets and a specials board written in chalk propped outside. He pushed open the red wooden door and walked in. He was surprised to find that it was already standing room only. What's more, inside everything was yellow and blue - Clifton Rangers' colours. After what seemed like an age, he managed to catch the landlord's eye.

"Alright guv'nor, you doing food?"

The landlord gestured sarcastically to an assortment of crisps, peanuts and pub snacks hanging on the wall.

Harry settled on a pint of John Smiths and a couple of packs of pork scratchings. He then found a space by the window and rested his drink on the sill. The atmosphere was building and at regular intervals a chant of "Bill Jameson's yellow and blue army!" would grow to a crescendo before dying away. Looking out of the window, Harry could see people making their way up the hill in the direction of Clifton Park, an almost continuous sea of yellow and blue. It wasn't long before he had finished his drink and "fine dining". Deciding against another long wait at the bar, he exited the pub and joined the throngs of fans. As he walked up the hill, he did notice one or two more knowledgeable fans giving him a "do-I-know-you" look, but each time he just moved on quickly through the crowd before they could place him.

The smell of burgers from the vendors hit him before the stadium came into view. Then the shops on either side of him fell away and he was able to make out the twin towers of Clifton Park. He had to stop and take in the full jaw-dropping majesty of what he saw. The whole side of the stadium was black reflective glass, flanked by two towers in the same style as the famous pair at Wembley. It seemed almost brand new – and most of it was. Bill Jameson had managed to convince the owner, Alan Salow, to invest practically his whole fortune into updating it. Across from the stadium on a large grass area Harry saw some fans who had erected tables and chairs and were drinking and eating food they had prepared beforehand. Harry wondered if these were fans who were unable to get tickets to the game.

Harry followed the signs to reception. Bill had left him a ticket for the game and a pass for the player's lounge for afterwards.

"Hi, I've come to pick up a ticket for Harry Welch," said Harry.

"Oh yes, our V.I.P," said the receptionist with an air of playfulness. "Bill will be so pleased you turned up; he's been worrying about it all day!"

Harry half-smiled, unsure if she was joking with him, but hoping she wasn't. She gave him both tickets in an envelope, and Harry set off to his seat. However, when he checked his ticket, he was surprised to see that his ticket wasn't for the seated section but for the terrace behind the goal. He was a bit disappointed at this as he had hoped he might get the full executive experience - prawn sandwiches and all!

He left reception and re-joined the fans making their way to the North Bank. There was a solid body of people at the entrance to the stand and it took him a good 20 minutes to gain entry. Unperturbed, Harry eventually took his place behind the goal with the Rangers fans. He was shocked again to see that, although there was still more than half an hour until kick-off, the stadium was already nearly full. Clifton Park had increased its capacity every year since Bill had joined, thanks in no small part to the owner's generosity, and now stood at 25,000 - an incredible 15,000 more than when Bill had first arrived. But the fans clearly believed in what Bill was building, and they had come in their droves almost from the moment he joined. Harry could have sworn there were at least 10,000 more than the official capacity there.

Harry took up a position to the side of the goal, where it was a little less crammed and a little calmer. Like all footballers, Harry was a fan at heart and was quite excited for the action to get under way. The fans cheered every Clifton player as they came out to do their warm-up - and booed every one of their opponents. Harry watched very closely. Clifton went about the warm-up in a business-like manner; it was clear they were very focused. They then went back off down the tunnel to do their final preparations and receive any last-minute instructions. Harry could imagine what it would be like in the changing room, with everyone going through their own pre-match routines and rituals. What he hadn't been prepared for was the wall of sound that greeted the players when they emerged again at 2:55. The whole stadium erupted. There was not one voice that didn't join in and even those in the posh seats stood up - forgetting their prawn sandwiches for a minute. The hairs on Harry's arms stood on end as he took a panoramic view of the stadium, taking in row after row of cheering fans. In no time, the whistle went for the game to begin, and Harry edged closer to the hardcore support immediately behind the goal.

By the time Clifton's second goal went in, midway through the second half, Harry was right in the thick of it, jumping around in celebration like everyone else. before he knew it, the final whistle had gone – it was a 3-0 win for the Rangers. He realised he was quite hoarse from all the shouting and singing. He couldn't quite put his finger on what it was, but he felt that he had truly been part of *something*. Standing there looking out over the pitch, it was like being a child again, wide-eyed with wonder at the beautiful game.

He then had to fight his way to the main stand, through the departing crowd heading in the opposite direction, before taking the lift to the players' lounge.

It's a strange thing for a manager, the end of the game. All the way up to kick-off, there is nothing else on their minds – planning, preparing, dealing with any issues, picking the team, changing the team, changing it again! Making sure that come kick-off, everything is perfect, and no stone has been left unturned. Not giving any player the slightest excuse for not performing to their optimum level. That's why the best managers are obsessive and controlling - never leaving even the slightest detail to chance. Once the game has started, they have less impact on things – perhaps just a slight re-organisation or well-judged substitution. Generally, most managers just find the 90 minutes stressful and will admit that during the match itself they are largely superfluous, other than at half-time.

Many people would picture the manager being at the centre of things after the game, but in fact many managers barely even speak to the players when it is over. They feel that they are too emotional at this point, too caught up in the drama of the game. Instead, they prefer to have time to think about and fully digest what happened, to get the opinions of others, to watch and analyse the videos before beginning to formulate a weekly plan based on what they saw. Any repercussions or difficult conversations can be had at the training ground during the week in a more non-confrontational way.

Bill Jameson was clearly one of those managers as no sooner had Harry reached the players' lounge than in walked the man himself. He had not actually met Bill Jameson in person until that day. He had spoken to him many times in the previous few weeks on the telephone, but this was his first time meeting him in the flesh. Before catching his eye, Harry quickly looked him over. He had cropped grey hair and was much smaller than Harry had imagined he would be. He was dressed in a blue shirt, black trousers and a yellow and blue striped club tie. He was, in short, physically wholly unremarkable. He may have been small in size, but he had a personality, an aura that filled the room. It was like someone flicking a switch.

Harry saw Bill scanning the room then spotting him. He had never felt so nervous in his entire life.

"Welcome to the club!" Bill said in a thick Scottish drawl.

With these three words, a relationship began – a relationship that was to change his life.

***

Harry stepped out of reception into the car park in a daze. The meeting with Bill had been a blur. Harry had felt almost bewitched by the wily Scotsman's words. The picture he had painted for Clifton Rangers was incredibly ambitious-yet Harry believed every word. He knew it would all come to pass. Even so, Harry had thought him cheeky at already having a contract drawn up. Bill knew that Rangers were Harry's last choice. Did he really expect him to sign it then and there?

It was easy to see his taxi as there were only a handful of cars left. The warm sun and blue sky had been replaced by a chilly night air and the only remaining light came from the moon. He lifted his collar and checked his watch. Ange was not going to be happy. He hurried over to the taxi and got in.

Up in his office, Bill was already faxing the contract to the league headquarters.

As the taxi passed the now shut Royal Oak, Harry pondered how he was going to let Ange know that he was now a Ranger for at least the next 5 years. Never mind the fact that he hadn't even discussed how much he was going to be paid. Nevertheless, he knew he had made the right choice.

It had never been about the money - not since the first moment he had stood on that crowded terrace on the North Bank. Anyway, the bonuses for collecting silverware were to prove very lucrative over the next few years. They won the Second Division in that very first season, and in his nine years working under Bill, Harry went on to win a further ten trophies, including four First Division championships. It all peaked on that magical night in Madrid when Martin Richards almost single-handedly destroyed Real Madrid and Bill Jameson's Rangers were crowned kings of Europe.

Chapter Three

Harry was brought back to the present by his phone ringing in his office, but he chose to ignore it. It should have been his day off. Harry's office was quite unusual in that it had a view of the pitch. This was another leftover from Bill's time at the club: he had told Alan Salow that he wanted to always have one eye on what was important. When the stadium was extended, he got his way. Harry wandered back across his office to his desk and sat down, still trying to ignore the phone. Surely they would give up soon. Kitted out in his well-worn Rangers tracksuit, he was running through in his head the previous day's humiliating defeat against fellow perennial strugglers Bartol City.

The '80s had been the worst decade in Rangers' history. It had seen them drop out of the top division, and although most experts had expected a quick return, it had never materialised. Now they were one of those clubs that were always battling at the wrong end of the table. This year had been no different.

His office was tiny but comfortable, and he sat at his desk holding a cup of cold coffee he had completely forgotten about, trying to work out a plan of action to get the club back where it should be. Most of the problems were obvious but there were so many of them he didn't even know where to start. He wasn't sure that some of them could even be fixed.

Mentally, the job was draining him. Physically, he was still in good shape, still at his match weight. Recently though, when he looked in the mirror, he couldn't help but notice the lines on his face, and the grey streaks that seemed to be multiplying in his hair - particularly fast since taking on the management role at the club.

In most people's eyes the blame for the club's demise lay firmly on one person's shoulders – the chairman, David

Salow. He had taken over the chairmanship from his much-loved father Alan two years to the day after that night in Madrid. Immediately, it became clear that to David Salow this was purely a business. One of the first things he did was slash the wage budget. After that, he cashed in on two of the club's most promising players. Corners were cut in almost every area, and gradually the club was eroded from within. Within the year Bill had retired, bad health meaning he no longer had the energy to fight the chairman. Harry was sold shortly after. Bill died in the summer of '81.

Harry himself had only been manager for just over two months, having started immediately before the start of the season. Incredibly, that was still longer than three of the previous thirteen managers the club had managed to work their way through in the previous 11 years. And even in the two months and six days that Harry had been in charge, he had found himself questioning his emotion-fuelled decision to take the reins at this club– could it become a millstone for him, he worried. Harry certainly didn't need the money; he'd been shrewd and invested his money wisely. Too many times he'd seen players blow their money with no thought for the future but he had quickly realised how short a footballer's career was. Half the players he'd played with at Clifton had used their money to buy pubs and bars; unfortunately they had all been far more successful on the customers' side of the bar. Many thought his acceptance of the club's offer was down to sentimentality. Perhaps... he considered. And yet Harry still had this nagging feeling...

It was true that the club only averaged 5,000 home fans these days, but he felt that if the club could get some sort of momentum going, the crowds would come creeping back out of the woodwork. If there was such a thing as a sleeping giant, then this surely was it. He had also felt he would be doing Bill a disservice if he didn't give it his best shot.

He also knew the players had potential and talent, and in Ryan McCoughlan he had a twenty-goal-a-season man. Earlier in his career he had looked destined for great things but distractions had come his way. Then there was Bradley

Carpenter - or Chippy as he was better known. Chippy had been capped three times for England at the beginning of his career, but - much like Rangers - his best days appeared to be behind him. He gave the impression that he was merely seeing out his contract with Rangers before looking for one more big pay day. Harry felt that both these players could be playing on a bigger stage, but that they were just drifting along, unable or unwilling to change course - like the Rangers. He felt the club just needed a spark, a catalyst that could resurrect the fortunes of this once great club.

Finally, he decided to give in and answer the damn phone - even if it was his day off.

"Hello," snapped Harry.

"Hello, can I speak to Harry Welch please?"

"This *is* Harry Welch. Who's this?"

"Sorry to bother you on a Sunday. My name's Len Carlton; I'm a scout for the club."

Len Carlton, thought Harry, that was a blast from the past. Harry had an excellent memory, and he could almost picture...

"Hello, hello, Harry… Are you still there?" said Len.

"Yes, I'm still here…"

That was it. They had a young lad join in training one day, and the lads were giving him a bit of stick. New players are seen as a threat; if they don't hit the floor running, a football club can be an unforgiving place. But Harry remembered this particular occasion for two reasons.

First because, unusually, it had been Bill who jumped in and stopped the session. Normally he wouldn't involve himself in player's squabbles, feeling it was all part of the path to excellence. But on that day he had said, in no uncertain terms, that the young player had been recommended by Len Carlton and that was good enough for him, which meant it should be good enough for everyone.

The second reason was that the young lad had ended up scoring a rather important goal in a European cup final a few years later. He had not heard Len's name in a *very* long time, and he didn't even know he worked for the club.

"-what can I do for you?"

Even before Len replied, Harry was already wondering if, just perhaps, he'd stumbled on the spark he was looking for...

Chapter Four

Nigel walked from the pitch with an arrogant smile from ear to ear. It could not have gone any better! The scout his dad had met in the pub the previous night had been there for four of his five goals. Nigel had spotted him straight away - he was exactly as his dad described him, even down to the cap.

"Don't miss me too much, lads!" he said to the rest of the team. "Do you want my autograph now? Before I get too famous!"

Nigel had always been flash; he was the biggest, strongest and quickest kid at Liam's old school, and he knew it. Liam had got used to ignoring his boasts, but this time every word was like a dagger. His whole life he had dreamed of being a footballer, and this dream was behind every decision he made. At school when his mates had started smoking, he had not. When his mates were going to parties and getting drunk at the weekend, he would be tucked up in bed saving his energy for the game the next day. Even girls had been a distraction he had avoided - although not always by choice!

He. Was. Obsessed. Every spare moment of every day was spent with a football at his feet. Deep inside he was sure he was good too. He really thought that he just needed a chance, an opportunity to really show people that he could be someone. The alternative was depressing: working at his uncle's garage for the next 50 years. At the moment, he worked there a few days a week and he knew that his uncle was keen for him to take on extra hours. But to Liam, every hour at his Uncle Gary's garage was an hour of football training he was missing - and another step down a road he did not want to travel. Today had been his big opportunity. He knew the scout was there to watch Nigel, not him, but he had decided he was going to do everything in his power to be noticed.

Well, that didn't happen, did it? It was 5-0 - and Nigel had scored all of them. He hadn't even had a shot on target. It was his own fault. He had a great chance to score about 60 minutes into the game, but instead of shooting, he had changed his mind at the last second and passed it to Nigel - who had promptly scored his fourth. It was shortly after this that he had seen the scout leave. At least it meant he had missed Nigel's fifth goal.

"Don't worry, lads, I won't forget you when I'm famous."

Liam had to go; he couldn't listen to Nigel for another second.

Liam picked up his sport holdall from the side of the pitch - there were no changing rooms on the marshes - and took out his own battered football. He intended to make use of the nets on the goals before the next teams turned up to claim the pitch as their own. When the next teams turned up, this was the cue for Liam to do what he normally did and try and find a game with another team. It being Sunday football, there would always be someone who didn't turn up, often because they were too hungover for a game of football. Then Liam would be in. These games were always eventful, even though the standard wasn't very high. Liam just saw them as another training session and he would work on his game, practising using his weaker foot, working on his long passes or anything else he felt needed improvement. Without him realising it, it also helped his awareness and strength.

There were other aspects of his game that improved in these matches too. Even though there were referees in these matches, they just wanted to get the game done, pocket their money and go home. Grievous bodily assault would have still received a shout of "play on" from the majority of referees. Liam, therefore, was always looking around him ready for any potential challenge. It meant that he always had a picture in his head of what was going on around him. He also became stronger, having to play against players who were a lot older and stronger than him. Although not the tallest, he was now deceptively strong and with his low centre of gravity, was very difficult to shrug off the ball. On the negative side playing in these games was the reason he had a strapping on his knee too.

Today, like most Sundays, one of the teams was short and so Liam found himself recruited for his second game of the day. He found himself playing for one of his more frequent foster teams, a team he affectionately knew as the Beer Belly 11.

It was getting dark as Liam finally left the marshes. He began to make his way home across the pitches towards the estate. As Liam walked, he became very aware of the time; he hoped his mum had saved him some dinner. His walk soon turned into a jog. Now he was hoping that his mum wasn't too cross with him. She wasn't exactly on board with the whole football thing, and he could do without the whole speech about working at his uncle's garage again. Gary was his mum's brother, which made things even worse. He only slowed momentarily at the sight of a Mercedes parked opposite his block. It was particularly noticeable amongst the old bangers and burnt-out wrecks of the estate.

He's brave, thought Liam as he slowed to a walk. He glanced inside the car to see if the owner had been stupid enough to leave anything on the seat, but he could see nothing through the tinted windows. He did notice a fresh key scratch down the driver's side though. Probably debt collectors or drug dealers, thought Liam - they were the only people on the estate able to afford this sort of car and brave enough to leave it unattended. He continued up the graffiti-littered, urine-ridden stairs towards the flat he shared with his mum.

Chapter Five

Uneasily, Harry checked his watch again. He had been here since about half past three and it was now nearly 6:30. It was growing obvious that he had outgrown his welcome; the stream of tea and biscuits that Mrs Osborne had been handing him had ended some time ago. Despite his obvious discomfort, Harry was determined to meet this prodigy that Len had so enthused about. Mrs Osborne was nice enough - some might even have called her attractive - but she had a hard, gritty air about her that suggested her life had not been without its share of hardship. The flat itself was basic but clean. The few pictures that he could see amongst the many ornaments were all of Liam, and Harry had noticed that in all of them there was also a football somewhere in shot. He also noticed that Liam's father didn't appear in any of them.

Liam recognised Harry as soon as he entered the living room. He was so star-struck and in awe that he didn't even register the severe scolding that his mum was now administering for his late return. Of course, he didn't have to listen too intently - it was a lecture that he had heard many times before. At least she didn't get onto his uncle's garage this time.

As soon as Harry felt Liam's mum had calmed down sufficiently, he took the opportunity to introduce himself.

"Hello Liam, it's a pleasure to *finally* meet you," he said with a wry smile. "My name is Harry-"

"-Welch" interrupted Liam, barely able to conceal his excitement. "You're the manager of Rangers, *and* you played in the European-Cup-winning side in '76!" he said.

"That's right," said Harry, who even after all these years was still caught slightly off-guard when anyone recognised him, "and the reason I am here today is on the recommendation of one of our scouts. I'm inviting you to play in a game for our youth team against Buxton Rovers at

Clifton Park on Tuesday night. It's an FA Youth Cup game. As you are clearly a fan, you will know how important that competition is to the club. Fortunately for you, Neil Harvey, one of our usual strikers, is suspended, so you'll be starting," finished Harry, feeling all this might be a lot of information for the star-struck Liam to take on board.

Liam didn't know what to say. An hour and a half ago he had been playing for the Beer Belly 11, and now here he was being asked to play for Rangers at Clifton Park!

"Well?" said Liam's mum, taking his hesitation for uncertainty and wanting to finally get this man out of her house.

"Of course I'll play!" said Liam, almost too quickly, not wanting to miss his chance. "I'd love to!"

"Great! See you on Tuesday night at 6:30; you'll need trousers, shirt and shoes. Just make your way to reception and tell them I sent you. They'll look after you. Whatever you do though, don't be late. Pat Waldron, the youth team manager, is a stickler for punctuality, and you *don't* want to start off on the wrong foot." Harry turned to Liam's mum, "Well, thanks very much for your time, Mrs Osborne - and for the tea. I'll make my own way out."

Harry started for the door, then turned and said "I know it's all been a bit out of the blue, Liam, but I've heard some very good things about you today. Make sure you prepare properly and don't take this opportunity for granted. Is there anything you want to ask me?"

"Is that your car downstairs?"

"Yeah, why?" said Harry. He hadn't been expecting that. "Err n-no reason…"

As Harry went back down the stairs, he couldn't help but feel a little sceptical. Liam had not been what he had been expecting. He was smaller than he thought he would be, and he also looked a little overweight. Could he really be the answer to his prayers and Rangers'? He seriously wondered if maybe Len Carlton had over-exaggerated his report on the young man. His mood did not improve on noticing the long, deep scratch going down the side of his new club car.

He also thought that Angie would not be too impressed either - he was supposed to have been home by two. Maybe Liam would not be the only one getting a scolding today.

Back upstairs, Liam still hadn't eaten, but he barely noticed his hunger. Far more important things were on his mind; he was really going to play for Rangers at Clifton Park - literally what he had been dreaming about for as long as he could remember. True, it was only the youth team, but he knew this was a start, and it was a start he intended to make the most of. There was something else on his mind too - he couldn't wait to see the look on Nigel's face when he gave him the news.

Chapter Six

Liam moved his boots to the back of his bag, refolded his towel and placed it next to his boots, and then slipped his shin pads down the side of his towel. He looked at it again, and this time put his boots at the front, the towel spread out on the bottom and his shin pads behind his boots. Then he shook his head and went to pick up his boots...

"Jesus! Leave it alone, babe!" said his mum, clearly exasperated.

"What? I just want to make sure everything's perfect."

"I know, but that's the fifth time I've seen you do that in the last ten minutes!"

Liam was about to argue the point, but then remembered he had been packing and unpacking his bag obsessively since Sunday, and decided against it. He had planned it all carefully: he was going to leave at 6:15, as he knew it was only a ten-minute walk to the stadium if he cut across the marshes. It was now five to six but he could not control his nervous energy anymore. He zipped up his bag and threw it over his shoulder.

"See you later, Mum, wish me luck."

"Good luck, babe."

Liam's mum looked at her watch and shook her head. She knew he would be early, but he was driving her crazy with his restlessness. Maybe it was a good idea that he got out the house - he'd been practically bouncing off the walls for the last two days. He was always bad before a game. He'd been like that for as long as she could remember. When he was a lot younger, he used to shake like a leaf as they walked across the marshes to his games. She had stopped watching him when he was about ten; she couldn't stand the drama if he lost. He would sulk for days, all over a game. Besides, by then she was having to work all the hours she could cleaning at the hospital, just to put food on the table and keep a roof over their heads.

Liam had on his old school shirt and trousers, and despite his best efforts his mop of blond hair looked just as unruly as ever. He had also been disappointed to see that in the five months since leaving school he had seemingly not grown at all. Both his shirt and trousers fit him just as well as they had the day he left. He certainly had no chance of making it as a goalkeeper.

He was soon at the ground, he approached from the right-hand side and crossed the road to the main entrance. He walked past the club shop, looking at the replica Rangers kits in the window, all of which seemed to be available at highly reduced prices. He then arrived at the main gate. This was a huge arched iron gate with the name of the club and some sort of Latin phrase moulded into the top of the arch. As he made his way under the arch, he entered the West Stand car park. Straight ahead was the reception. Liam knew this part of the ground well: he had often waited here after the game, trying to get players' autographs. Written across the West Stand in huge silver letters, each of them bigger than Liam, was "Clifton Park Home of the Rangers". It seemed strange to be here now, with the car park almost empty and without the murmur and movement of the crowd. He felt different too. Normally he came here as a fan, but today was different. Today it was like going behind the scenes on a studio tour.

He was early – obviously - so he spent his surplus time wandering around the magnificent stadium, trying to imagine what it must have been like during the club's glory years; he had never even seen the stadium half-full. Although he felt positive about being there, he was well aware that it could be over very quickly, and he wanted to savour every second. Over the previous 48 hours, he had pictured this evening in many ways. The overriding feeling, the one that excited him more than any other, was the idea that he was going to be part of this club - even if perhaps just for one night.

At 6:20 he made his way back to the club reception. He pressed the buzzer outside the door and a click let him know he could enter. Taking a deep breath, he entered the marble entrance hall. The first thing he noticed was the full-size black-and-white photos of Rangers greats. He knew them all, and in his head he silently named them. Behind a few leather seats he saw the reception, where two receptionists were sitting behind tinted glass. At that point the sound of a sliding window alerted Liam to the fact that one of the receptionists was ready and waiting, complete with a welcoming smile.

"Hello, can I help you?" said the receptionist, looking quizzically at Liam, who seemed to be in a world of his own.

"Mmmm, yes, err… sorry, I was told to, I mean, err… Harry Welch said, Pat Waldron…" said Liam incoherently, like a tourist trying to ask for directions in a foreign land - he was about as successful too!

The receptionist had on a plain white blouse, her hair was clipped back, and she had on very little make-up. It was as if she had deliberately set out to look as conservative and plain as possible. If so, thought Liam, she had failed. Her friendliness radiated from her eyes and Liam was grateful for her warm welcoming smile.

"You must be Liam Osborne? Mr Welch asked me if I would deliver you safely"

"Yes, sorry," said Liam. "That's me, Osborne… I mean… I'm a little bit nervous," he added unnecessarily.

"That's OK," laughed the receptionist – who, Liam could now see from her name tag, was called Lisa. "It's better than half the young players we get. Most of them act like they're far too good to talk to anyone."

Lisa then opened a side door and came out from behind her enclosure. She led Liam back through the reception area to a door next to a flight of stairs and a great glass elevator. As she walked, Liam was surprised to find himself looking her up and down. He mentally reminded himself of the need for focus. She entered a code into a brass keypad on the wall next to the door, then opened it wide for Liam to enter.

Liam stopped in his tracks. At the end of the white corridor ahead, he could see the hallowed turf of Clifton Park. He was slightly below pitch level but could just about make out the first few rows of the East Stand.

Lisa turned to show Liam into the home changing room, but saw he was no longer with her. Confused, she looked back down the tunnel and saw him standing there, mouth wide open, staring straight ahead. Once again, she couldn't help but laugh out loud at this peculiar boy.

"Hey, don't forget why you're here! We can give you the tour later!"

Liam returned her smile, secretly hoping the bit about the tour was true, and hurriedly re-joined Lisa. She knocked on the door, and it was opened by a stern-looking man with a prominent nose who impatiently waved them both in.

"Hello, Mr Waldron. This is the player that Harry asked along. He told me you would be expecting him."

Pat Waldron nodded curtly and gestured for Liam to step inside, barely glancing in his direction. Lisa gave him one last smile of encouragement, then departed back up the tunnel.

Liam slowly entered the changing room, then waited, nervously looking around. In the middle of the room was a padded treatment table with a smaller table next to it. By the tables was a curious-looking man. He was short and fat, with a bald head and thick milk-bottle-bottom glasses. He was wearing a Rangers tracksuit, but it looked old and did not fit him too well. He was placing drinks, oils, chewing gum and rolls of electrical tape onto the table. He reminded Liam of a cartoon character. Liam smiled and nodded in his direction but in return all he got was a grunt.

Around the edge of the room hung the famous yellow shirts of Rangers, numbers showing. On benches below them were pairs of socks, shorts, warm-up tops and tracksuits, all neatly folded. On the wall was a huge whiteboard with a pitch marked out in black tape. On the pitch the numbers one to 11 were set out in a four-four-two formation, and under each number was the name of a player.

Liam was relieved, although a little daunted, to notice that his name really was in the starting 11; he also noted he would be playing up front with someone called Jarvis.

Standing by the whiteboard was a third, more athletic-looking man with short white hair, wearing Rangers shorts, socks and a training top with the initials AK sewn on. He was busy taping up sheets of paper: lists of penalty takers, free-kick takers, and organisation for attacking and defending set pieces. As he put them up, he checked them carefully against a list of the team.

"Right, Liam…" said Pat, finally facing Liam. "The others are just on their way down - the YTS boys have been having tea and toast in one of the function rooms upstairs. Put your bag under the number ten. I'll introduce you when the others get here."

When he had finished, Pat motioned with his arm towards a space below the number ten shirt, not even bothering to introduce Liam to the other two men. Liam sat down, feeling a bit apprehensive about meeting the other players. But before he could dwell on it for too long, the door swung open and in came the rest of the team. Instantly, Liam felt out of his depth and had an almost uncontrollable urge to leave. There was he in his old school uniform, still with what his mum charitably described as "puppy fat". The young men - for that's what they were - who walked, almost swaggered in could not have been more different.

First, it was the way they dressed. Everything they wore had a designer label, from their Farrah trousers and Ralph Lauren shirts to their Wallabee shoes. Then the way they held themselves. They strode into the changing rooms with their heads held high, radiating confidence, speaking in loud and brash voices. It was like every one of them had been produced on an athlete production line, each a virtual clone of the other.

Liam knew he did not belong.

"Right, gentlemen, hurry along and find your place. We have a lot to get through and we need to get our minds on it early doors," said Pat.

The boys checked the team sheet on the board, before making their way to their spaces on the benches. One or two looked disappointed when they looked at the board, a few others looked happy. Liam tried not to catch anyone's eye as the players took their seats and was pleased that no one sat down opposite him. He could tell by their body language that they also knew he did not belong.

"Right, settle down. It's a big game for us today but before we get started, I would just like to introduce a new face." He gestured towards Liam. "This is Liam Osborne. He's a striker, and he comes recommended from up high. Now, ordinarily a new player wouldn't go straight into the first team, but the powers that be have *instructed* me to make an exception. Neil's suspended, so we do have a space, although I sympathise with those of you on the bench. Still... try to make him welcome and help him through the game. This will be very different to what he's used to. He's never played at this level before." Pat turned to the boy with ginger hair next to Liam. "Try and talk him through the game the best you can."

Liam sat staring at a spot on the floor a metre from his feet. He couldn't believe what he had just heard. If Pat's intention had been to alienate Liam from the rest of the team, then he had clearly succeeded; the other players had been left in no doubt about their manager's opinion on him. This was not going how Liam had pictured it.

Without pausing, Pat went on to discuss what he expected from each player, as well as what he wanted from the team as a whole. If Liam was being honest, he would have to admit that much of what was said went straight over his head - a lot of it seemed to be based on things they had worked on in training. But he still listened intently, trying to take in as much as possible.

"Right boys, you have 20 minutes to get ready and to then be out on the pitch with Alex for the warmup." Said Pat nodding towards the white-haired man who seemed to offer a half-smile to Liam, but Liam did not notice.

The bald man started strapping ankles on the treatment table. A few players went up.

"Johnny, mate, can you do my left ankle?" said a particularly tall boy with long brown hair, a long white face and a West Country drawl. Johnny just grunted in reply, which the tall boy took as a yes. He sat up on the treatment table so Johnny could start to apply the strapping. Players were taping over rings, sniffing smelling salts and any number of things he had never seen before. He got changed quickly, trying to blend into the background. He then went to put his boots on.

"They're filthy!" said Jarvis, getting Liam to push them back down in his bag. "Try and sneak them on outside, otherwise you'll be fined for sure."

To Liam they did not seem dirty at all; he always banged the mud off after playing and gave them a wipe-down. But looking around, he saw that everyone else's boots were pristine. Liam wondered how he could be fined when he wasn't getting paid any money, but he did what he was told, grateful for some advice, and consequently found himself out on the pitch before any of the other players. As he slipped on his boots, it was all he could do to contain himself. The grass was immaculate - it looked like it had been manicured, not mowed. The contrast to what he was used to brought a smile to his face. As he stepped onto the turf, he looked all around him at the towering stands, turning full circle. The stadium looked so different from pitch-level. In fact, the pitch almost seemed to arc slightly so the two sides were fractionally lower than the middle. He bent down on one knee and brushed the palm of his hand across the surface, feeling the wetness from the sprinklers spraying onto his sleeve. He then closed his eyes for a second, imagining the hum of the crowd, before rising to his full height and testing out both the grass and his footwear with a few short sprints and turns.

Gradually, he was joined by the other players, both from his team and the opposition. They started jogging around and moving from side to side. Liam kept waiting for a ball to arrive, but one never did. Then Alex came running out with some orange cones. He used them to set up a little grid on the side of the pitch, before calling over the team. They all jogged over and spent the next twenty minutes in a series of rhythmic movements interspersed with running and various stretches. Then finally they got out the footballs and split into smaller groups to begin getting a feel for the ball, and gradually introduce longer passes and quicker movements. The other boys were clearly familiar with the routine and seemed to cope easily with the warm-up, but Liam, who was more used to just turning up and playing, found it very difficult. He was often out of breath, and usually a pace or two behind the other boys. This was a rather inauspicious introduction for Liam and did not go unnoticed. Pat was standing to the side watching the warm-up, and was not impressed with what he was seeing. He glanced up pointedly at the executive boxes, where he could just make out a familiar figure watching.

About fifteen minutes before kick-off, Pat called them in, and all the boys ran over and down the tunnel into the changing room. Liam followed but already felt a little heavy-legged. The atmosphere in the changing room was hugely different to earlier. The players seemed much more animated as they did their final preparations, taking on liquids and putting on their shin pads - some of them even doing their hair by throwing on water from the drinking bottles. They moved around offering words of encouragement, shaking hands, giving high-fives and slapping each other on the back. Pat and Alex shouted out last-minute reminders above the hullaballoo. Liam was largely left alone, so he concentrated on positioning his shin pads correctly, adjusting his boots then changing out of his warm-up top and into his club shirt. As he slipped the shirt over his head, he caught sight of the badge. Suddenly, he felt his emotions rising. It was true that up to this point things hadn't exactly gone to plan, but as he saw himself wearing the shirt of *his* Rangers, suddenly the magnitude of what was happening overcame him. He swallowed hard, trying to stay in control. He made himself breathe slowly, gradually getting his emotions under control, not wanting anyone to see what wearing the shirt, the badge meant to him. He knew he couldn't lose this opportunity.

He was brought back out of his thoughts by one or two of the players giving him some last-second encouragement and slaps on the back - although he wasn't sure that they realised it was him they were encouraging. Then a bell rang, and everyone lined up, ready to go out onto the pitch. A few players moved along the line to get to their favoured places. Some were waiting before putting on their shirts, a first introduction for Liam to the superstitious world of sports. Pat opened the door and both he and Alex ushered the boys out of the changing room and onto the pitch.

Chapter Seven

Liam looked around. Even though they were about to kick off, the ground was empty apart from about a hundred people in the West Stand - presumably family of the players. He didn't care though - to him it could not have meant more if there had been 50,000 watching. The referee blew his whistle and both captains made their way forward to shake hands, toss the coin and choose ends. Clifton Rangers' captain was Jason "Blackie" Blackmore, the long-faced boy who'd had his left ankle strapped by Johnny. He promptly won the toss, so they didn't change ends, and Rovers kicked off.

After twenty minutes, Liam was exhausted, even though he had barely had a kick. His legs felt like they were on fire and he was having problems catching his breath. In the games he had played in the past, he had always decided when to run and when not to, but this was different. It soon became apparent that when the ball went to certain places on the pitch, he was expected to be in a certain place too. For example, when the Rangers' left-back got the ball, he had to move to the left side of the pitch, get between his opponent and the ball and then be available for the pass to his feet. But if Jarvis was closest and got there first then he would do that instead, and that meant that Liam would be expected to make a long run in behind the Rovers' defence towards their goal, hoping for a long pass over the top. Then if it went to the right-back, they had to do the same thing but on the other side of the pitch. The worst was when Rangers passed the ball from one side to the other, as this meant he and Jarvis had to sprint to get to the other side on time.

It felt like he was continuously on the move. It was like he was a remote-control toy being controlled by Jarvis, who would tell him where to go and when. Most of the time, when he made the run, the ball didn't even come in his direction. Then if he got too tired and couldn't make the run, inevitably the ball went to where he should have been, and he received a mouthful from Pat on the bench as well as from half his team. When he did happen to make the right run at the right time and the ball came towards him, the defenders were quicker, stronger and fitter. They would either beat him in the race to the ball or simply shrug him off it. He felt like he was on a merry-go-round and couldn't get off. And so, it continued...

When the half-time whistle went, Liam wished the famous ground would just open up and swallow him. He was embarrassed by his performance. Maybe his mum was right - maybe he should just ask his uncle to make him full-time at the garage. What made him think that he could play football for a living anyway? He felt completely out of his depth. Time to stop with his crazy dreams. The score was still 0-0, but he'd made no difference to the proceedings at all - unless it was a negative one.

He made his way back into the changing room and slumped down, exhausted physically and mentally. He could see some of the players talking in whispers and looking in his direction - he dreaded to think what they were saying. Once everyone was seated, Pat began to talk. His team talk was fairly positive, mainly reminding them what a big game this was and that at 0-0 there was still all to play for. He gave instructions to all the players individually. When he came to Liam, he informed him that he had another fifteen minutes and if things did not improve, then he was going to *have* to take him off. All Liam could do was nod. He agreed totally: if he had been the manager, he would probably have already taken him off! As Pat spoke, Liam sat there, thinking that something had to change - but what? He knew he couldn't continue as he was, but he also knew that he couldn't do all that was being asked of him.

When Pat had finished, he turned to Jarvis.

"I'm struggling out there; I can't keep up. How about you make the runs in behind and I just show to feet? There's no point me trying to get in behind. I'm just too slow."

Jarvis did not look too impressed. He obviously saw this as Liam getting him to do his work for him, but he agreed anyway. He knew that things weren't working as they were.

Before he knew it, Liam found himself back out on the pitch, ready for the second half. The first time the ball came his way, he tried to control it, but the defender marking Liam had already decided that he wasn't worth worrying too much about. Rather than defend properly, he gambled and got in front of Liam to take the ball just as Liam was trying to control it. The defender passed it into his midfield, then gave Liam a look of contempt. On the side-line Pat held his head in his hands, as did a couple of Liam's own team out on the pitch. Up in the executive box Harry picked up the phone and with a heavy heart dialled the dugout.

The phone rang in the dugout, and a few moments later Pat sent the substitute forward out to warm up - ready to come on. This was all unbeknown to Liam, who was himself plotting *his* next move...

Not having to make so many runs meant that Liam was a little more in control of his body and mind. Rovers were on the attack, but Liam had already positioned himself in front of the defender - just in case the ball came his way. At that moment, Jason Blackmore, who was clearly Rangers' best player, made another clearance. The ball made its way towards Liam. Liam had a quick glance over his shoulder and saw the defender looking to repeat his last trick. Not this time, thought Liam. As the defender came past Liam's left shoulder, Liam used his body to block his run. Instead of controlling the ball, he let it run between his legs. The defender was now on the wrong side of him, while Liam had the ball and was facing the opponent's goal. His only real passing option was Jarvis, who was about 20 yards in front of him and was still running towards the other team's goal. Liam took another touch but was aware of the defender recovering, using his superior physical attributes to make amends for his mistake. Liam had to do something, and quick! With the outside of his foot he passed the ball into space for Jarvis to run onto. He was clean through on goal, or at least he would have been… Unfortunately, Jarvis had no idea that Liam was capable of such a thing and so had stopped his run. The goalkeeper was able to nonchalantly jog off his line and collect the ball. But Liam knew that his pass had been a good one, and he took encouragement from that fact.

Rovers' next attack was ended sharply by another towering header from Jason Blackmore. The ball came out of the stratosphere towards Liam, who was already in position again. His marker was a little more cautious this time, unsure if Liam had meant the ball to go through his legs before, and stood a few yards off. Liam had already spotted that he had a little space. Despite the height the ball was coming from, he controlled it instantly and passed the ball to the now more alert Jarvis.

As this happened, the phone in the dugout rang again. The Rangers' sub returned to his place on the bench, as did the scowl to Pat's face.

For the next 15 minutes Liam had the beating of the Buxton defender every which way. If the defender stayed off him, then he would control the ball and invariably find a teammate, while if the defender got close, he would simply pass the ball first time, finding clever little angles to create space for his teammates. And if the defender got cute and tried to nick the ball from in front of Liam, then he would just turn him and find the ever-willing Jarvis.

The Rovers' defender was getting more and more frustrated. Then, as Liam was controlling another difficult pass, the defender ran at him and kept running - straight through the back of Liam. Liam collapsed to the floor, the wind knocked out of him. As the referee reached inside his pocket to pull out the yellow card, Liam slowly tried to rise to his feet. But it soon became apparent that he was finished for the day. The substitute forward was sent to warm up again and within a few minutes the number ten board was held aloft to signify the end of Liam's game.

Liam slowly made his way across the field to the bench, every step seeming more painful than the last. He slumped onto the bench. Pat didn't say a word to him. Some of the players on the bench did offer some words of encouragement, while Alex remarked that he had, "shown some nice touches". His mood was not helped when the substitute who had replaced him popped up with what proved to be the winning goal with ten minutes to go. He felt deflated when the final whistle went, despite his improved second half, wondering again whether he was really up to this level of football. It was cushioned a little by the knowledge that he had played a part in their passage to the next round of what was, after all, the biggest youth competition in the country.

When the whistle blew for the end of the game, Alex came onto the pitch and called together all the players, including the substitutes, and began the cool-down. Liam struggled through it; 15 minutes sitting on the bench had left him stiff as a board. But it only lasted a few minutes and then Alex sent them back to the changing room. As Liam approached the tunnel, he could see Pat and Harry Welch having what looked like a heated argument. Harry was straight in Liam's eyeline, and so, feeling slightly awkward, he put his head down and quickly made his way into the changing room. On seeing Liam, they finished their conversation and Pat followed Liam into the changing room, while Harry continued up the corridor.

Back in the home changing room, Pat began dissecting the game, praising some players and criticising others but not mentioning Liam's contribution at all. This wasn't something that Liam took as a very positive sign, especially when the player who replaced him was congratulated for making such a difference. Pat then told the players to shower and change, giving instructions to some of them who had specific jobs, like doing the kit and cleaning the changing room. Tomorrow was a day off for recovery, he told them, but they were meeting on Thursday at 8:00 a.m. for Johnny's bus, and they should *not* be late. Then almost as an afterthought, Pat turned to Liam and asked him to wait in reception when he was changed and ready. He needed to speak to him.

Liam took a deep breath. He felt sick.

Once he was changed, he made his way out of the changing rooms and up the tunnel. When he got to the end, instead of opening the door and re-entering the reception area, he stopped, turned and looked back out towards the pitch. Liam felt it was one of the most stunning views he had ever seen, and he was all too aware that this might be the last time he got a chance to see it from this angle. Then, feeling his emotions rising again, he turned, opened the door and went and sat in one of the chairs by the glass table. As he sat there, he saw every one of the players leave, laughing and joking together and being met by their families - all in stark contrast to him. He also saw Pat disappear into the elevator without even glancing in his direction. Before long, lights began to go out around the stadium. Liam got more and more nervous, and he started to wonder if Pat had forgotten him. If he hadn't, how much longer would it be before the moment he was now dreading would arrive? All this time, he was unaware of the pretty receptionist, still sat behind the tinted glass, looking on with pity at this slumped, unhappy figure. She had already seen many hopeful young boys with their dreams in tatters. This one seemed different though, and she really felt his pain and anguish. She wanted to give him some kind of advice or inspiration, but she was unable to find the words or the courage.

So there he sat, alone with his thoughts, until he heard the winding of the lift. He saw the metal doors slide open to reveal a waiting Pat, who called for him to come with him. His face gave no clue as to what was to come. Liam instinctively glanced back to the reception, perhaps sensing someone watching him, perhaps in the hope of seeing a friendly face, but he couldn't see anyone there. He dragged himself up from the chair and solemnly made his way to the lift, like a convicted killer taking his final walk to the gallows.

They went up three floors in silence. Despite the seriousness of his position, Liam was looking all around, trying to spot something of interest. But this was mainly an administrative floor and so he didn't see much that interested him. Pat ushered him into a room which had a sign saying "Youth Team Manager" on the door.

"Have a seat," said Pat, sitting down behind his desk.

Liam tentatively sat. The youth team manager leaned back, tapping his fingers on the desk as if deep in thought.

"Right," he started, looking intently at Liam. "You, young man, are a conundrum. You have talent; there is no doubt about *that*…"

Liam's heart lifted a little.

"*But* I am not sure whether that is enough. You aren't fit enough, strong enough or quick enough to play at this level."

Liam's heart dropped again.

"And what is worse is that in the second half you didn't play for the team, but for yourself. You made Jarvis do the work for you and then just grabbed the rewards and that, *that* is inexcusable in my opinion. *However*, you clearly have friends in high places: Mr Welch seems to believe that your talent could be enough, and that you may be worth a gamble."

Pat paused, staring into space for a moment, apparently gathering his thoughts. Liam just sat there, waiting to see what the outcome was going to be.

"So here it is. We have agreed that you have up to and including our next FA Youth Cup match to prove to me that you are worthy of this opportunity. Today is 21st October and the next round is on 5th December, six weeks away.' You will have until then to change my mind. But I warn you now, if your performances have not improved drastically by then, you will be out the door. During this time, you will receive £29 a week, do all the training that the other YTS boys do and will be available for selection for all the youth team games. Whoever your guardian is will receive £50 a week as housekeeping for the six weeks you are here. There's no training tomorrow, so you need to be at the ground on Thursday morning for an eight o'clock departure. You will need nothing except your toiletries; everything else is provided - including clean boots. Do you understand?"

Liam just nodded. He was trying to process all the information he had just received and trying not to think too much about the significance of the clean boot comment.

"Right, that's all. We'll see you Thursday - and don't be late."

Pat looked away from Liam to check something on his computer screen. This clearly signified that the meeting was over.

Liam rose from the chair and made his way back into the lift then out through reception in a kind of daze, still processing the information he had just been given. He was unaware, as he did so, of a pair of sympathetic and very concerned eyes watching him intently for clues as to the outcome of his meeting. They did not have to wait long. Seconds after he left the reception area and entered the car park he double-pumped his fists in relief and cried "Get in there, you beauty!"

Lisa smiled to herself. Maybe she would be seeing more of this curious young man after all.

Chapter Eight

When Liam finally awoke, his head was still spinning from the events of the previous night and his whole body ached from the exertions of the game. But he had something else on his mind.

He had told his mum what had happened when he got in, leaving out some of the more challenging parts of the night. She had actually been very positive about it, especially when he explained about the housekeeping and the money he would be getting paid.

"Talking of money, you need to go and see your uncle Gary in the morning. He'll be expecting you for work tomorrow."

"Do I have to?" said Liam, "You know what he gets like. Can't you tell him?"

"Course not. You need to tell him, I'm sure he'll be fine with it…"

Both she and Liam knew he wouldn't be.

***

"Hi Liam. Why are you not in your overalls?" said Gary, sliding out from under the Ford Capri he was working on.

Liam had been working for Gary since leaving school, mainly doing menial jobs like cleaning, mopping up and lugging boxes. He knew his uncle was struggling and needed him to work more hours, not fewer.

"Hi Gaz, I need to talk to you about something…" said Liam, trying to sound as breezy as possible.

He briefly went through the events of the last few days, hoping his enthusiasm might placate Gary a little. It didn't work.

"So that's it. You know how busy I am and now I'm going to have to do everything myself! And for what? So you can go have fun playing at footballers," said Gary.

"It's not just playing. I'm getting paid, and they're giving Mum some money."

"Oh, do me a favour, Liam. You must know that the football YTS is just a made-up scheme. The government likes it 'cause they get you off the dole, and the clubs like it 'cause they don't have to pay out any money! Everyone wins, 'cept the poor kids on the scheme: they can chuck you out whenever they want but you can't leave without their permission. It's a scam, Liam. Barry's boy had the same thing going on. Look at 'im now - out on his ear. You're like a slave; they'll have you cleaning the ground and painting the walls."

Liam glanced towards the mop and then at his uncle.

"It's my dream, Gaz - you know that. I've got to give it a go."

"Well don't think I'm gonna keep your job waiting for you. If you leave now, you might not have a job to come back to." With that, Gary slid back under the Capri.

"Cheers, Uncle Gary. Thanks for the support," said Liam. "Maybe you should just give Barry's boy a call!"

Gary made no response, just carried on repairing the Capri as if Liam wasn't even there. Great, thought Liam, now I know why Mum didn't want to tell him.

He spent the rest of the day resting and trying to let his body recover. He couldn't believe that a game of football could affect him like this. He didn't get any sympathy from his mum, who thought it hilarious that her 16-year-old son was moving around the flat like an old-age pensioner.

"Jesus, Liam, you'd better be moving better than that tomorrow or you won't last till the end of the week!" she said laughing.

Liam didn't find it funny.

That night in bed, he found himself staring at the ceiling and running over all the future possibilities. He was acutely aware that he needed to get some sleep, but there was one thought he could not get out of his head - his one huge nagging doubt: was he good enough? He hadn't exactly set the world alight in the game on Tuesday, and Pat had been quite scathing about his show in the second half, even though Liam had thought that was his strongest section of the game. Ever since he had left the car park on Tuesday night, he had been running through all the different scenarios that could take place over the next six weeks. He had so many worries and concerns but at the same time knew so little of what to expect. It made it impossible for him to really focus on what he had to do. The only thing he knew for sure was that the next six weeks were going to be the most important of his life so far. At about three in the morning, he finally drifted off.

Chapter Nine

His alarm woke him at 6:00 a.m., and although he hadn't long been asleep, the adrenalin had him up and out of bed in seconds. Even though he knew it was important to have breakfast, the butterflies in his tummy meant he couldn't eat a thing, and once again he found himself ready to leave far too early. He tried to kill an hour watching the saviour of breakfast TV, Roland Rat, on TV-am - not that he saw much as he was constantly checking the clock. In the end he left at 7:30 and arrived at the ground a full 20 minutes early. When he arrived, he realised he had forgotten the toiletries bag his mum had put together for him.

It was probably a good idea to be early - with it being the first day, he was sure there would be a lot to sort out. He was disappointed to see that Lisa was not on duty, but the receptionist who was there was nice enough and sent him off in the direction of the tunnel, having first entered the code by the door, then giving him directions to the kit room. When he got there, he saw Johnny. He was up to his knees in dirty kit and was stuffing it into a series of washing machines. He was even smaller than Liam remembered. He appeared to still be wearing the same tracksuit as Tuesday night and was definitely wearing the same scowl. Liam was a bit scared.

Johnny turned around, stopped what he was doing, then stared at Liam, hands on his hips. After a few uncomfortable seconds, Liam realised that this was his cue to talk.

"Hi, my name's Liam. It's my first day."

"Size?" said Johnny.

"Sorry?" replied Liam.

"Boots," said Johnny.

"Eight. I'm a size eight, sir." said Liam in reply.

Johnny then disappeared around a corner and returned with two boxes containing brand-new pairs of Umbro studded and moulded boots. He proceeded to dump these into Liam's arms before turning back to his work as if Liam was no longer there. Liam was getting used to being treated like this so he thought he would oblige, leaving the kit room and quickly returning to reception.

When he got there, several of the other boys from Tuesday night were there sitting in the chairs by the glass table. The captain Jason nodded in Liam's direction. No one else even acknowledged him. They were all dressed, clone-like, in tracksuit bottoms and Adidas Gazelle trainers, with polo shirts hidden under large padded coats. Liam felt out of place in his old school uniform.

He sat down and commenced staring at the floor again, trying not to get involved in any conversations and wishing the time away. The conversations he heard were all about nights out and girls - two things he didn't know much about anyway.

At 7:57, a minibus pulled up outside the doors. Johnny clambered down from the driver seat, entered the reception area and went off down the tunnel. A minute later he returned with a large hamper-style padlocked skip on wheels, presumably full of kit. Without a word, he put the skip in the back of the bus. Simultaneously, the boys made their way out and onto the bus and sat down in what seemed like pre-determined seats, leaving only a few free for Liam to choose from. No sooner had he made his selection than Johnny got on board the bus and started to drive away. It was dead on 8:00am.

As he got to the gate two boys came running down from the right, shouting and waving at him to stop. Liam recognised one of them as the substitute from Tuesday night, Lee Hodges, but Johnny just pulled straight out as if he hadn't seen them. He clearly had seen them - it was impossible not to. He turned left, then continued down the hill onto the high street. All the boys rose from their seats and began to bang on the windows, laughing and jeering at the unfortunate boys, who had already started heading off towards the bus stop to begin their alternative journey to the training ground. This clearly wasn't the first time this had happened.

The rest of the journey was uneventful, but boisterous. The boys in the youth team had clearly already formed friendships. Liam sat alone. One of their pastimes could only be described as Johnny-baiting. The idea of the game was to ring the bell on the bus as many times as you could in one go without Johnny spotting you. From what Liam could gather listening to the accompanying banter, the forfeit for getting caught was Johnny pulling over and chucking you off the bus. As a result, most of the players tended to play after training so as not to risk being late for training and accruing a fine. But the serious players still had a bit of a go on the way. Liam had to admit it was quite amusing and time passed quickly watching the other youth team players play the games to shouts of "Five's the record!" or, after one particularly impressive effort, "Seven's the record!" This was intended to further rile the victim of their amusement, who could often be heard cursing under his breath at the "little buggers".

The training ground was about a 20-minute journey, although it was only about four miles as the crow flies. The main building was a large Victorian house that had been converted so that downstairs there were two large changing rooms, each with their own shower block. The first team changed in the room to the right, and the reserves changed in the room to the left - or at least they would have if the ever-frugal millionaire chairman, David Salow, had not shut down the reserve side to save money the year after the club was relegated.

To the right of the house was a path, which ran past a little pond to another basic wooden hut where the YTS boys changed and where all the footballs, cones, bibs and boots for training were kept. Further on was a Portakabin where the medical team were placed, with a basic weights room in the rear including weights and several exercise bikes. Behind the buildings was a huge and beautifully maintained grass field with four football pitches and various grids marked out on it.

The minibus pulled into the training ground and drove up to the YTS huts on the edge of the field. The huts had two separate rooms, and the one on the right was where they got changed. It was a long room, basic and badly lit, with a communal shower area at the end, and it reminded Liam of his old school's changing room. The room was freezing cold, with no visible heating. There were already a few players there, who had obviously made their own way to the training ground. The boys from the bus entered the room to laughter and a few jeers, then sat down at what were clearly their usual places. Liam sat in a spare space, waiting to find out what to do.

The door flew open and Johnny entered, dumping the skip in the middle of the room, then unlocking it, flinging open the lid and leaving. The boys all jumped forward and frantically grabbed the towels inside, rolled up with kit in them, trying to find the kit in the best condition, often emptying a towel before searching for alternative socks or shorts. Before long the boys who had missed the bus arrived and they were stuck with whatever kit was left strewn across the floor.

Once everyone had changed, they made their way out of the changing room and back in through the door on the left. This room was full of football boots hanging on numbered hooks. Each boy grabbed a pair of boots from the numbered pegs and moved to the front table, where there were brushes and polish to clean them. These were the first-team players' boots - each YTS player was allocated a player's boots to look after. Liam, feeling a bit of a spare part, asked Jarvis if he needed a hand and was soon cleaning one of his boots. At the back of this room in the communal showers were about 80 footballs, all piled up together. Liam noticed that when a couple of the boys had finished their boots, they began cleaning the footballs in the shower. Once Jarvis had finished cleaning his boots, he grabbed the other one off Liam and led him towards the big house.

Liam tried to start up a conversation with Jarvis as they walked up the path, but Jarvis was obviously not a morning person. They left the boots on the steps to the house so the first team could grab them on their way in, and went to the urn that stood outside the dining room to get a cup of tea. Shortly after, all the other boys began to make their way up from the huts. It was about 9:30 by now and as Liam stood there drinking his tea, he was treated to the sight of the first-team players beginning to turn up.

Liam stood there in awe for about 15 minutes as his tea went cold - like a giddy schoolboy, which is pretty much what he was. He barely noticed Jarvis wander off to join some of the other YTS boys. The YTS players had got a football out of a ball bag and were starting to organise a game.

But Liam was oblivious to everything as he saw Rangers' two star players turn up: Ryan McCoughlan, then Bradley Carpenter, Liam's favourite Clifton player. Carrying their designer wash bags, they picked their boots up off the step before disappearing into their changing rooms. It made everything all the more real for Liam, as well as all the more frightening. Once they had all gone into their changing room, Liam joined the other YTS boys with the footballs. They made a circle and passed the ball around the outside while the two players in the middle tried to win the ball. Apparently, the game was called piggy, presumably after piggy in the middle. Liam found it quite tough at first, as the players were all quicker than he anticipated, and they seemed to get to balls that Liam thought they had no chance of reaching. But as they went on he caught up with the pace more and more. After the first few minutes, during which he gave it away a few times, and had to become one of the defenders in the middle, he didn't give the ball away at all and was starting to feel a bit more confident.

Every now and then Liam would glance back over towards the house and was quite surprised to notice that none of the first-team players seemed too interested in the footballs. They spent most their time talking on their phones. Mobile phones had just started to become popular, although they weren't too mobile yet.

It looked like training was almost ready to start, but some players were only just turning up. He was even more surprised to notice that several of the first-team players, including Ryan McCoughlan, were smoking cigarettes. They had just dropped into the relegation places on Saturday, and he couldn't help but think that they did not seem particularly eager to put things right.

The game of piggy was halted by the shouts of Pat Waldron and Doug Clemance, the first-team coach, calling their players in and over to their designated areas. Doug Clemance was a huge man, with massive hands and a thick beard. He looked like Father Christmas if he were a WWE wrestler. He had played in goal for England more than 50 times, and it had been considered a coup for Harry when it had been announced that he was going to be Clifton's new coach. The first-team players went over to the pitch out in front of the car park, while the youth team made their way to the pitches on the left in front of the dining room.

Alex was already on the pitch when they got there and he had set up some sort of training session, with cones placed around the pitch. Meanwhile, on the first-team pitch there was another coach, who Liam didn't recognise, helping Doug Clemance by setting up a drill on the pitch, while Doug took the players on a slow jog around all the pitches. Harry, like most managers at the highest level, rarely came out onto the training ground.

As soon as the YTS players got to the pitch, Alex got them to line up in twos and started taking them on a warmup all the way around the field, same as the first team was also doing. Well, Alex said it was a warmup, but to Liam it was a living hell!

"Keep up!' said Jason, Liam's partner, practically dragging him along.

"Right lads when I blow the whistle the back 2 need to sprint to the front," said Alex.

Every time the whistle blew for Liam and Jason's turn to sprint from the back, he had to fight the voice in his head telling him to quit. It felt like his legs did not have anything left to give. If it was not for Jason, he would not have made it. When it finally finished, they stopped for some stretching. Liam just stood there with his hands on his knees gasping for air while everyone else stretched. Then they were off for three more laps of the same thing but quicker.

"Liam!" shouted Jason back over his shoulder.

The whistle went and Jason was off.

"I-I can't." said Liam.

The rest of the team carried on with the final lap. Liam could see them up ahead, all of them still running with strength and power. Liam lowered himself to one knee and tried to control his breathing. He could sense the first team squad coming up behind him and his shame made him rise back to his feet. He knew he couldn't face being overtaken by his heroes. By now the YTS boys were three quarters of the way around the field. Liam slowly cut across the middle of the field and joined the squad just as they started their second set of stretches.

Liam was spent while the other boys seemed to be barely out of breath. He joined in with the stretches but could see some of them whispering and knew that he was the subject of the conversation. He stood alone too embarrassed to join back in with Jason, trying not to catch Alex's eye. He felt he had let him down. Eventually Alex called them all over.

The training session itself was very enlightening, as it was defence versus attack and involved Pat regularly stopping the practice and telling people where they should be and what runs they should be making. Again, the other boys seemed to have a basic understanding of what was expected, but for Liam it was all new. Unperturbed, he tried to take it all on board, and the more he was shown, the more he wanted to know. Physically though, it was a problem; he had an aptitude for the movements and passing patterns, but he could not keep up with the demands of the movements he had to make. Several times he could see the other boys getting annoyed when he was not where he was supposed to be, and a couple of times he saw Pat shaking his head when he could not quite keep up with what was going on. Alex, on the other hand, was far more understanding and praised him a few times for catching on so quickly.

When they had finished, they had a cool-down with Alex - three more laps! Thankfully for Liam this was more of a slow jog and had many stops for stretches. They then had a bit of a pep talk from Pat, in which he explained that tomorrow would be another light session! They then had to collect up the balls and make their way back in to get changed.

The first team had long finished and could be seen leaving and making their way down to their overpriced sports cars and Range Rovers. The only exception was Chippy, who had stayed out after the rest of the first team had gone in to practice his free kicks, as he often did. The boys who had taken the ball bags out in the morning now had to collect up all the footballs that had been used in the morning sessions and return them to the hut next to the YTS changing room, counting them as they did so and tracking down any that were missing.

While they were changing back into their normal clothes, Jason Blackmore came and sat down next to Liam. Liam was relieved that Jason seemed to already have moved on from what happened in training, unlike some of the other players. He explained that Pat had told him, in his role as captain, to hand out a job to Liam. Apparently, all the players were given jobs they had to do, that they then rotated every month. Jason said that on Saturday, he was to stay behind after the first-team game to clean the changing room. Jason seemed a little surprised to see the smile on Liam's face when he was told of the job because it was one of the harder, dirtier jobs, and most the YTS boys tried to steer clear of it. But for Liam, any chance to be around the changing rooms on a match day sounded thrilling.

"How do I get into the changing rooms?" Liam asked, rather too enthusiastically.

"Right mate, you get a ticket for the first-team game and a pass for the players' lounge after our game on Saturday morning. Then you simply walk around and into the tunnel when the game is finished. I've given you that job as it is the one I'm doing this month, so I'll be able to show you the ropes myself."

"Saturday morning? Does that mean we play on the pitch before the first team game?"

"No, we only play at the ground if we have a midweek cup game - like Tuesday," Jason said. "Normally we play here, then Johnny takes us back to watch the game if the first team are at home."

Once they were changed, they went down to the dinner hut to grab a bit of lunch. Outside the main house, Liam saw all the first-team players' boots dumped on the floor, caked in mud. The YTS boys then had to take them down to the boot room after lunch, before catching the bus back to the ground.

The next day followed a very similar routine: from the morning meet at the ground and the bus journey through the cleaning of the boots, the morning tea and a quick game of piggy, and then again a long warm-up. Though on this occasion they did not go back to their respective area straight away. Instead, they stopped by the first-team pitch.

"What's going on, Blackie?" Liam asked Jason, who seemed to be the friendliest of what was increasingly appearing to be an unfriendly group.

"The day before a game we take on the roles of the next opposition, so the first team can run through their set pieces."

Liam became very nervous and very excited at the same time. He would be playing on the same pitch as his idols, even if it was in the guise of the enemy. It was something he had long dreamed about.

He had to wait a while though. First of all, Doug ran through their attacking set pieces, for which they only needed the youth team goalkeeper, defenders and midfielders. Liam watched as Doug and the other coach,

Ray, walked around with a clipboard of notes and diagrams, pushing and pulling people into place as they did their free-kicks, throw-ins and corners.

Liam was fascinated. It felt like being a spy, watching all the secret moves that were going to be put into place against Wiltford on Saturday. Wiltford were having a great season and were in fourth place in the Second division, so for Clifton this was going to be a very tough game. After about 40 minutes, the first team moved onto defending free-kicks, and Liam, Jarvis, Lee Hodges and Neil Harvey were sent in to take the place of the Wiltford attack. A couple of the bigger boys, Jason being one of them, were to be the Wiltford defenders who went forward for free kicks.

Liam was to be Steve Whelan, the Wiltford striker who had already scored eight goals this season. He was being marked by Reggie Stephens, Rangers' tough-tackling veteran full-back. Reggie was shaven-headed and had a permanent look of annoyance at the world; he had a reputation for being "over-enthusiastic" in the tackle. For the most part Liam just had to make near-post runs, as this was what the scouts had said that Steve Whelan did on free kicks out wide.

The ball never really went close to Liam, and he found himself getting more and more frustrated with Reggie Stephens: despite the ball being elsewhere, he kept digging Liam in the back or grabbing his shirt as he went to make his run. On about the twelfth go, the ball was played towards Liam and he controlled it instantly. Reggie was kicking and niggling at him, but Liam had had enough. As if banishing all his frustrations in one swift movement, he dragged the ball on the inside of his foot and swept it through Reggie's legs. He then collected the ball on the other side, to a couple of shouts of "olé!" from amused first-team players. Liam was preparing to shoot but just then Reggie took a two-footed lunge at his calves, and the shot hit the side-netting. Liam crumpled in a heap to the sound of laughter from the other players. Reggie was already above him, spitting and snarling and telling him what he would do to him next time if he ever tried to make him look stupid again, the words interlaced with a variety of swear words a couple of which Liam didn't even recognise. Liam slowly rose to his feet, tested the steadiness of his legs and spent the rest of the practice hoping the ball would come nowhere near him!

At the end of the session, after the cooldown, Alex called Liam over. As they walked back towards the house, he put his arm around him.

"Great play out there, laddie, but why did you stop? It looked like you didn't even want the ball at the end."

"Do you blame me?" said Liam. "He nearly snapped me in half out there; I thought we were supposed to be playing for the same club!"

"Look, Liam, you need to get your head around things quickly. Reggie's 31; he has a mortgage and three kids. His contract's up at the end of the year. Every day at this club is a battle for him to keep a roof over his head, so if he lets some trainee take liberties, then he might as well give up now. It's dog eat dog at a football club, and the only mistake you made was you let him intimidate you."

"Well, what was I supposed to do? Punch him? He would have eaten me alive!"

"No, laddie, don't you get it? You play to your strengths. Reggie was scared of you. Not that you might hurt him, but that you might embarrass him - and that's worse. Stick to what you're good at and don't let other people dictate to you," said Alex, before jogging off.

When Liam got back to the changing rooms, Pat was waiting, and all the boys were sitting on the benches.

"Sit down," instructed Pat. "OK then, tomorrow's game is at nine o'clock. Meet here for a 10:30 kick-off. For those meeting at the ground: Johnny is leaving at 8:30. Don't be late, or you all know what will happen."

At this, there were a few rueful smiles from several of the boys, who had obviously been left behind by Johnny in the past.

"It will be the same squad as Tuesday, as Neil is serving the last game of his ban, so an early night for everyone please."

With that, he left, making his way back up to the house.

Great, thought Liam. Neil Harvey is back after Saturday. That means there will be four of us fighting for two places. If I don't put in a good performance on Saturday, I might not get another opportunity.

Chapter Ten

The journey to the game was uneventful and they all clambered out the minibus at ten to nine. Liam followed the other boys down to the pitch, next to where the first team trained. It was roped off; the grass had clearly been newly cut, and there were still sprinklers spraying water on it. Once there, the boys wandered around the pitch. As always there was a high level of banter, but you could see some players were already in matchday mode - a little quieter, a little more intense. Liam watched everything closely trying to take in every moment.

The pre-match ritual was much the same as Tuesday night, just transferred to a different venue. The Rangers' youth team changed in the first-team changing room, while Wiltford used what used to be the reserve team changing room. Liam was relieved to see his name on the team sheet, still with the number ten. Before long, he was out on the pitch and warming up. He was still struggling a little from the demands of the week and his legs felt quite tight. There was also a couple of grazes on the back of his calf, courtesy of Reggie. The warmup seemed to be even more demanding than Tuesday night. Mercifully, it wasn't long before they were being called back in for their last-minute preparations and instructions, then sent back out on to the pitch for kick-off.

If he thought Tuesday night had been hard, it was nothing compared to today. If anything, it was even more frustrating, as now he knew where he should be; he just could not seem to get there in time. On several occasions he made what would have been great runs but he lacked any sort of explosiveness, which meant the defenders were able to recover and stop any danger. Added to this was the fact that this time Jarvis seemed determined that Liam would do his fair share. This meant that he often had to try and spin in behind, in the forlorn hope that he might reach a ball that he knew was out of his reach, but this only meant he was even more tired out the next time it came his way.

In the first 45 minutes, Liam probably touched the ball four times. Twice, his legs felt so heavy that, although his control was good, he still had to overstretch to get the ball on his second touch, and it was all he could do to poke the ball to a teammate. On the third occasion, he flicked the ball through; he thought the pass had been excellent but was disappointed to see that no one had made the run he had expected, and the ball ran through unchallenged to the opposition goalkeeper. The fourth time, he managed to pull an almost unreachable ball out of the sky, and from fully 30 yards unleashed a dipping shot that only just failed to dip in time and only just cleared the bar. But that was it - the rest of the half was just an exercise in pure futility; he seemed to be treading water in his own personal nightmare. It didn't help that his own teammates saw him as a suitable scapegoat and took every opportunity to chastise him on his poor play. The look on Pat's face every time Liam didn't get to the ball didn't help either; his head would shake like maracas at almost everything Liam tried.

At half-time, the boys made their way back to the changing rooms. Liam sat ashen-faced, once more staring at the floor. Pat came in and gave his half-time talk, which again was quite encouraging for the most part. He then turned to Lee Hodges and told him to get ready, as he would be coming on for Liam. Liam's heart felt like it was in his mouth; he fought to keep the tears from welling up in his eyes. He felt like an imposter as he slowly changed back into his old school clothes, while the rest of the team made their way out for the second half. He then sat there for a few moments, his head in his hands, steeling himself for the humiliation of walking out having only played half the game. After taking a few minutes sitting alone in the deserted changing room, he followed the boys back out to the pitch, where he took refuge, hidden amongst the trees, to watch the second half.

Alex was troubled. It was true that Liam was struggling physically but he had seen moments from him that had taken his breath away. But he also knew that in his role as assistant manager he had to support Pat fully, even if his heart was telling him they could be making a massive mistake. He glanced over at Liam, trying to blend in amongst the trees, and decided he would have to do something. A talent like this did not come along often. Now, though, he had to decide what…

The second half did little to make Liam feel better, as the YTS boys went on to win 3-0, with Jarvis scoring twice and Lee Hodges getting the other. The rest of the morning was a blur. The team got changed and were given their tickets for the game, as well as a pass for the players' lounge, and they made their way onto the bus to head back to watch the first team. Liam was also given his weekly wages by Alex: £29 in cash in a small brown envelope. He was almost too ashamed to take the money.

When they got to the ground, he followed the other boys into the reception. The rest of the team all dispersed. Some went to the café to get something to eat, courtesy of the club; a few went to the players' lounge to put on a bet; one or two even made their way outside to sell their tickets to one of the ticket touts patrolling out by the iron gate, and some went to do their jobs around the ground. In no time, Liam found himself standing in reception with Jarvis. It was awkward. Liam felt Jarvis had hung him out to dry in the game, and he wanted to know why.

"Thanks for that," said Liam.

"What?" said Jarvis.

"You know what. You knew I couldn't make those runs - you practically sacrificed me out there."

"Who the hell do you think you are?" said Jarvis loudly. "Why should I let you do all your fancy touches while I do all your work for you?"

Jarvis then left through the main doors, leaving Liam alone in every possible way.

Liam stood there, distraught. As the people in reception all turned to face him, wondering what the noise was, he could feel himself welling up for the second time that day. At that moment he just wished he could beam himself back to the marshes, before any of this had happened. Luckily for him, out of nowhere he felt someone taking him by the sleeve and leading him through a door behind the tinted glass of the reception, out of the public glare.

"You OK? What was all that about?" said Lisa, looking intently into Liam's anguished face.

"I just want to go. I can't do this. I shouldn't be here!" sobbed Liam, now unable to hold back the tears.

"Look, just tell me all about it. Believe me, I've seen most things at this club. I may be able to help."

Before he knew it, he was telling Lisa everything. He didn't know if it was the pressure of the last few days, or if she was just a good listener, but something made him trust her. He told her about the talk with Pat, the incident with Reggie, how cold the boys had been and the latest flashpoint with Jarvis. When he had finished, he looked back up at Lisa, relieved to have got it all off his chest.

"You're right, Liam. You haven't been treated well and it sounds awful, but... that's football," she said. "It's not like you read about in comics or see on the TV. It is a brutal, cruel game. This is real life. Do you know how many YTS boys have become professionals here in the last two years?" She paused to give Liam just enough time to shake his head. "One. Billy Butler. And he has only played twice for the first team since then. If you start feeling sorry for yourself, then you might as well walk out the door and go home now. Get your head right. Once you do, everything else will fall into place. At the end of the day, no one owes you anything."

This was not what Liam had wanted to hear. He had opened his heart and what did he get back? Walk out the door and go home!

"Thanks for nothing!" he said over his shoulder as he left the room.

Lisa stood there, staring after him. Maybe she had been a little harsh, but she knew what she was talking about - and for some reason she couldn't bear to see him fail without even having given it his best shot. She returned to her window to deal with the queue of people wanting her help, but her thoughts were still with Liam and they stayed that way for the remainder of her shift and into her evening.

As Liam left the room, part of him wanted to do exactly what she had said. But he saw Jason heading for the door to the tunnel, so set off after him.

"Hey, Blackie, wait up!"

Jason turned and smiled awkwardly at Liam, strategically ignoring his puffy red eyes. He then took Liam down the tunnel and to the side of the pitch. Once there, Jason walked along the dirt track at pitch side, before being let into his seat by one of the stewards, who obviously recognised him. Liam just walked behind, in a daze. Pitch-side on a match day. This whole experience had him in a spin. One minute he was almost breaking down in public - the next, another huge high. The proverbial rollercoaster ride. He almost had to pinch himself. As he took his seat, he could see everyone looking at him like he was someone important.

"Here, sit next to me," said Jason, obviously feeling sorry for Liam after the morning. "A lot of the lads will have sold their tickets to the touts outside. I don't think there'll be many others from the team"

Once again Liam was shocked: free tickets at pitch side for the first team and they don't even show! It was slowly becoming clear to him that the real world of football was very different from the romanticised view he had.

The game itself didn't do much to improve his mood. Rangers were beaten 3-0 and Steve Whelan got two goals - neither of which were from free kicks or corners, Liam was pleased to note. The biggest highlight for the crowd was when Reggie sent the Wiltford winger over the barrier in one particularly hefty challenge. Liam winced in sympathy. Other than that, Rangers went down with little more than a whimper. Despite his awful day, he still felt privileged to have seen his Rangers in action - even more so now he felt he knew a little more of the people behind the famous faces.

At the end of the game, Jason took Liam back round to the tunnel and they waited for everyone to change and leave, so they could clean the changing room. Liam was surprised to see so many of the Rangers' players leave smiling and joking. He felt that such a loss should have hurt them more. Reggie was one of the few players who still looked upset at the loss, and this was confirmed by the rather graphic comment he aimed at Liam and Jason when they offered some encouragement. When everyone had left, they went and stood at the changing room door. Liam gasped - there was mud and tape everywhere, and half-eaten sandwiches on every available surface. There were dirty towels and jock straps all over the floor and the whole room stank of a mixture of sweat, Deep Heat and overpriced cologne.

"Right, mate, best get started!" said Jason in his thick West Country accent.

No kidding, thought Liam.

They began by picking up all the tape off the floor and putting all the rubbish in a black sack. Next was the uncomfortable job of picking up the discarded jock straps and putting them in the laundry basket. This was all done under Jason's instruction, as he had obviously done it a few times before. When they had cleared the floor, Liam stood back and looked. The floor was filthy; it would take them ages to mop it.

"Don't worry," said Jason, throwing the bucket of water into the middle of the floor, much to Liam's bewilderment. "I have a plan."

He then threw the used towels that they had collected on top of the water. Next, he stood on top of the towels, so that they were lodged below his feet. Jason then proceeded to ice-skate around the room, the towels as his makeshift skates, cleaning the floor in the process. Liam soon joined him, and a right picture they painted, the two of them skating around like Torvill and Dean! It was the first time

Liam had smiled all day. The smiles turned to laughter as they added theatrical arm movements to their routine, now fully into the parts they had invented. When they had finished and stopped laughing, they put the towels into the skip, which they then returned to the laundry room, eventually heading back up the tunnel. As they went their own ways Jason stopped and turned to Liam.

"Look, mate, it's not even been a week yet. Don't let them get to you. What do you think it was like when I first started? Do you hear anyone else with this accent? I was the butt of everyone's jokes - all tractors and sheep. You just have to dig in, believe me. Everything is soon forgotten when you start playing well."

With that, he went on his way, leaving Liam in the middle of the car park. Liam stood there for a moment, thinking hard about what Jason had just said. A pang of guilt momentarily made him turn back towards reception, but he changed his mind and decided to put the day behind him.

Chapter Eleven

The rest of the weekend seemed to pass all too quickly, and Liam soon found himself back on the minibus and on his way to training. The mood was a lot quieter and more sombre; it soon became clear that this was because, with no mid-week game, the boys had two full days, morning and afternoons of running and hard work to look forward to. This filled Liam with dread - the "easy" days had been a big enough struggle for him.

The dread shown by the other boys was not misplaced: Monday and Tuesday, they did not even *see* a ball. Liam could not believe there were so many torturous ways that a group of people could run and punish their bodies. Groans met every announcement of the next method of cruel and unusual punishment. Doggies, bleep tests, pyramids, box-to-boxes, increase and demand - and each worse than the one before.

Liam was sick twice on the Monday and three times on Tuesday. He was also the only boy who did not complete every exercise. No fewer than six times over the two days, Liam admitted defeat and sat out an activity that he felt he was unable to finish. Again, this did nothing to endear him to the other boys. After training on Tuesday by the time he had got back to the YTS huts he found his clothes all over the floor in amongst the water from the showers and mud from the boots. The other boys obviously did not feel he was pulling his weight. As he picked them up, he could feel the tears coming. He fought to control himself, he knew he couldn't break down in front of everyone. The humiliation would be too much...

"Here mate, let me help."

With Jason's help Liam soon had his clothes back on his peg.

His walk back home from the ground took just over 30 minutes due to the stabbing onset of cramp every two minutes. What was worse was that halfway home he realised he needed the toilet. When he finally got to his building, he was desperate. He stood at the bottom of the stairs, staring upwards. There was no way he could get up the stairs in time, and since he had never known the lift to work in all the years he had lived there, he had no choice but to add his own scent to the smell on the stairs.

One week down, thought Liam, and I am probably worse off than when I started.

Wednesday was a day off and Liam stayed in bed *all* day, except to take a long bath, before retiring early in preparation for another day of hell. Liam's mum was baffled by the whole thing: the Liam she knew was a hyperactive bundle of energy who never sat still. What worried her more was the cloud that seemed to hang over her son's head. No amount of coaxing by her could get to the bottom of it; she just had to hope it was something that would work itself out.

The Thursday and Friday went by without much incident. They actually almost seemed like "easy" days now. When they went up against the first team on Friday, Liam did his best to avoid the ball and so the day passed without incident.

That session was the final straw for Alex, and after training he put things into action.

Chapter Twelve

Len got off the number 96 bus and took the short walk to the training ground. At the gate to the training ground the security guard looked at his worn, dog-eared pass closely, before reluctantly letting him through. The game had already started, and, as he got to the side of the pitch, he soon noticed that Liam was standing on the touch line in his tracksuit; he had obviously not been selected for the game.

The game itself was a huge disappointment to Len - all pace and power but no finesse. With 15 minutes left, Liam came on for the Rangers' number ten, a rather aggressive forward who had already been booked and looked on his way to a red card. With the other players a little tired from their already considerable efforts, Liam was able to get to one or two balls that he would not have managed in previous matches, but it was obvious to Len that he was both low on confidence and not at the same level of fitness as the other players. Nonetheless, in the short time he was on the pitch he still had more moments of quality than many of the other players, and Len saw nothing that changed his original judgement. He did, though, agree with his old protégé's diagnosis that something had to be done. There were four and a half weeks to go, and if things did not change then Liam would be leaving as quickly as he joined. Len left at the final whistle, giving himself a chance to get a step ahead of Liam. There was something he wanted to show him.

Liam got off Johnny's bus and started to make his way towards the exit, dejected by the small amount of football he had played, and at the chance he could now see slipping through his fingers. When he got to the gate, he saw an old man dressed in a sheepskin jacket, with an old flat cap perched on his head. He appeared to be waiting for someone. He looked familiar to Liam, but he couldn't quite place him.

"Hello Liam," said the man.

"Hello. I'm sorry, do I know you?" said Liam.

"No, but I know you. My name is Len Carlton and I am the reason that you are in this mess!" Len said. "Alex told me that things were not going to plan. He thought I might be able to assist..."

Len beckoned for Liam to come with him, and he led him back into the stadium, through the main entrance and into the lift. As he went through the reception, Liam put his head down. He was still avoiding Lisa. Once they were in the lift, Len pressed the button for the fourth floor.

Len then continued down the corridor, before stopping at a black-and-white picture of the European-Cup-winning side. They were sitting on the pitch in Madrid, with the trophy on the floor in the middle of them. Len pointed at one of the players.

"Do you recognise anyone?" he said.

Liam looked closely but couldn't quite make anyone out...

"Imagine less hair and greyer"

"It's Alex!" said Liam, then looked at the names at the bottom of the picture. "But... but that's Alex Kempster. People say he was the most skilful player ever to play for this club. I didn't realise that he was *our* Alex!"

"That is correct. The Wizard, they used to call him. You should have seen him playing on the marshes when he was your age. Nothing of him, but his feet were so quick..."

"You mean?"

"That's right, Liam. I brought him to the club - just like I did you. Back then, it wasn't about how big or quick you were but about what you could do with the ball - and Alex, he had feet like hands. There was nothing he couldn't do with a football. But do you know what, Liam?"

Len turned to Liam and looked him square in the face.

"Even with his God-given ability, Alex worked like no other. I remember I used to see him every night on the marshes rain or shine, running and doing press-ups and sit-ups until he could no longer lift his arms. Even after he was signed. First one at the training ground and the last one to leave. It didn't matter to him how hard he got kicked; he just got up and demanded the ball, again and again and again."

At this, Liam thought back to his recent run-in with Reggie Stephens. He was suddenly embarrassed.

"Because you know what, Liam? Ability is nothing without heart and desire. You have this talent that puts you ahead of everyone else, because they can never do the things you do - but it's not enough by itself. Do you understand what I am saying?"

Liam looked from Len to the picture on the wall and back to Len. He could see the passion in this old man's eyes, and it shamed him.

"I... I understand," he replied sincerely.

As they made their way back down in the lift, Liam made plans with Len to set things right. Len also told him of another unlikely old friend of his who could help Liam, and promised he would put the wheels in motion. When they got to the gate, Liam thanked Len and promised he wouldn't let him down.

"Are you off home now, Liam?"

Liam glanced over his shoulder, back towards reception.

"First I just need to go and apologise to somebody who also gave me some great advice."

Chapter Thirteen

Lisa was more than happy to accept his apology, but she looked him up and down and told him it was on one condition…

***

"Hey, Liam, over here!" shouted Lisa, waving her arms to get his attention.

She looked very different from how she had working at reception. Her hair was down; when not tied up, it was quite curly and reached about halfway down her back. She had on an oversized light-blue sweater, tight black leggings and sneakers, and beige leg warmers covering her ankles. Liam saw her through the shoppers walking by and returned her wave.

"Hey Lisa, you look… great!" said Liam, practically tripping over his own tongue.

He was dressed in an old pair of jeans and had on a grey sweatshirt. He had spent ages deciding what to wear, but in all honesty, he didn't have too much choice, as he had never really had much interest in clothes. But then, of course, that was why he was here.

"Is that a compliment? Why, Mr Osborne, you'll make me blush!" She nudged Liam in the side, while laughing at his obvious discomfort.

"Whatever. Come on then, what's the plan?" said Liam.

"Don't look so worried. This will be fun. First off, we need to get you some everyday clothes. Then we'll get you something a bit more appropriate for your matchday outfit. Can't have you looking like someone out on a class trip every time you turn up for a game!"

This time it was Liam's turn to nudge *her* in the ribs.

"So you're like my P.A. for the day then? OK, I can handle that."

"Don't push your luck, Osborne!" said Lisa, as she put her arm through his and led him off to Clifton's only department store.

Against all his instincts, he did actually enjoy himself, something he found hard to believe, considering he was doing two of his least favourite things: shopping and talking to girls. Lisa had been great fun to be around. Even if she did spend most the day teasing him about his taste in clothes and dropping huge hints about his need for a haircut! Once again, he'd found himself really opening up, in a way which was alien to him; he even briefly spoke about his father, and that was something he never did. But everything had seemed so natural. Liam didn't know if he had a type; he couldn't say he had ever considered it before, but if he did, she was it. He couldn't remember the last time he had laughed so much; it certainly hadn't been since starting his trial at Clifton. As for the shopping, the plethora of bags hanging off his wrists were evidence to how easy that had been. He'd had his £29 and his mum had given him the £50 the club had given her too. Coupled with the money he'd saved from working at his uncle's garage, it all came to a nice little wedge - or at least it had, because his pockets were now a great deal lighter!

Lisa was also having a surprisingly enjoyable day. She had been worried about crossing that line between her personal and professional life, but there was something about Liam that fascinated her and drew her in. She had been a little guarded about her own private life, but Liam hadn't noticed - he was far too busy buying up half of Clifton High Street. When it got to about one o'clock, she realised that she really needed to get going. She had a Sunday shift at the club that evening, and she had to go home and get ready.

"Is that the time?" said Lisa, "Wow, it's flown by Osborne, spending your money has been more fun than I thought!"

"Don't get used to it," Said Liam laughing.

"Ok… next time I'll let you spend it on me instead! I saw some great shoes in Clarkes! They were only £150…" Lisa laughed, "Don't worry Osborne I'm only joking- don't want you breaking down again!"

"That's harsh!" said Liam, trying to look hurt but failing.

"What? Too soon Osborne? Seriously though I do need to go, I need to get changed before work."

Can I walk you home?" asked Liam, regretting that his little shopping expedition was coming to an end.

"Err… no, that's OK, thanks, Liam. Those bags look heavy. I'll see you at the club in the week." She reached forward and gave Liam a peck on the cheek, giggling at his almost immediate flush.

Then she was off. Liam watched her admiringly as she went. He had really enjoyed his day. His mind was bubbling with questions. What exactly was going on with him and Lisa? Were they just friends? Was there any chance of something more? She was the only person at the club who had really gone out of their way for him from Day One. He trusted her ahead of anyone, and trusting people was not something he did easily. He snapped himself out of his daydream, realising that this was no time for distractions. Now more than ever, he knew what he wanted and how to get it. He was determined to be single-minded in his pursuit. His feelings for Lisa were going to have to wait. He had been pushed around enough. Starting tomorrow, he was going to start pushing back.

Chapter Fourteen

On the bus into training on Monday, there was once again a general sense of dread at the running that was in store for them over the next couple of days. Liam, however, did not feel any dread - he couldn't wait to get started. He knew this was just a necessary step along the road on his journey, and he now relished the challenge that it was going to bring. His mindset was such that he actually hoped it would be harder than last week. The other players had already sensed a change in Liam, and not just that in his newly bought attire, he seemed to be much less out of place - Lisa had done a great job.

This new attitude came off him in waves and spread into the training. Although he was still sick twice on the Monday and once on the Tuesday, none of the activities defeated him. Every time he felt he could not go on, he dug deep inside himself and was surprised to find a steel and determination he did not know he had. In fact, he briefly led on the box-to-box run on the Tuesday, and although most of the other players clawed back his lead and overtook him, for the first time he was not last. He did the same in the pyramid run.

After training on both the Monday and the Tuesday, he did not get the bus back with the other boys. Instead, he gave his own clothes to Jason to take back to the ground for him, and ran the four miles all the way back to the ground. True, he did not run very fast, but despite his exertions of the day he never stopped.

On the Monday he continued through to the kit room to see Johnny.

"Hi Johnny. Len said I should come and see you," he said. He was nervous; Johnny still had that effect on him.

Johnny looked up from his pile of washing, disdain on his face – although, to be fair, Liam was not sure if he had any other look.

"This way!" he said.

Liam followed Johnny all the way back out into the car park, where they turned right and headed towards an old building, still within the grounds of the stadium. Len pulled out a set of keys and opened the door. They entered a huge brick room, with no windows and dirt on the floor. At either end were two old iron five-a-side goals cemented into the floor. On the walls there were various chalk targets.

"The ball court," barked Johnny, as if it needed an introduction.

Len had already told him about it. Apparently, this was where the first team used to train under Bill Jameson before the training ground was built, and they still used it if it was snowing or the pitches were waterlogged.

Johnny led Liam up the stairs into a weights room. It didn't have any new-fangled machines, just old-fashioned barbells and an exercise bike. Johnny threw a set of new keys in Liam's direction and left.

On both the Monday and Tuesday, it was dark when Liam finally left. Each time he did, he locked up, made his way through the reception to the shower and changed back into his own clothes, before heading for home.

"Hey stranger," said a voice, as he left on the Tuesday.

"Well if it isn't my P.A," said Liam in reply.

Lisa laughed and stepped out from behind the screen.

"P.A? More like a stylist! Look at you in your new togs."

Lisa walked over to Liam, grabbed him by the hand and span him around, theatrically checking out his outfit.

"Not bad at all, Mr Osborne, not bad at all."

She then laughed to see that she had made him blush once again.

"Hello. Excuse me, miss, are you the receptionist? Can you help me?"

The voice caught them both by surprise, as did the fact that they were still holding hands. Lisa quickly dropped

Liam's hand, turning to the man who had interrupted them both.

"Sorry, sir, I'll be right with you," said Lisa, as she quickly made her way back to reception.

Liam stood there motionless for a moment, then gave Lisa a wave over the man's shoulder before making his way home, an extra skip in his step.

Wednesday was a day off, but not for Liam. Even though his legs were aching and his muscles tight, he jogged to the ground and made his way down the tunnel, past a security guard. He nodded and smiled at this young man, who had seemed to practically be living at the ground over the past few days. When he got to the end of the tunnel, he got the set of keys out of his pocket and unlocked the gate leading out onto the pitch. He stood there for a few moments, taking in the sight in front of him. He saw Clifton Park as a holy place - his church, if you want, and he stood there breathing it all in.

He then started by doing a couple of warmup laps of the small dirt track encircling the pitch, before stretching. He then looked at the large clock on the main stand; 9:47, he mentally noted, before setting off. He set himself a target of 20 laps in the next 30 minutes - that would be about a minute and a half a lap, which he knew was quite a challenging time, as his warmup laps were taking over two minutes each.

At 10:19 he finished his twentieth lap. He was disappointed to see that he had just missed out on his target. To make up for it, he worked extra hard in the weight room, before "borrowing a ball" from the kit room and spending a couple of hours striking the ball at the various targets on the ball court, using every part of both his feet, controlling the ball impeccably before the strikes. Len had told him that Martin Richards used to spend hours in the ball court, striking the ball at the targets. One of Len's favourite Martin Richards stories was to do with those targets in the ball court.

Rangers had just got a new coach who was trying too hard to impress in one of his first sessions.

"Right," said the new coach. "I want you to hit the ball onto the round target with your left foot, then control it with your right foot, onto your chest, up to your head, back down to your right foot, then volley it into the square, before controlling it with your thigh and then catching it on your left foot."

As Len told it, all the players just cracked up at this ridiculously complex set of instructions. Except Martin Richards, who just stepped up. Left foot - circle – right foot – chest – head – foot – volley - square – thigh - catch on left foot. Bang, exactly as the coach had said.

"You mean like that?" he said, casually turning to the coach and the rest of the team.

The team fell about laughing, and it was just more fuel for the Martin Richard legend. As for the coach, he took it well and went on to be a very big part of the Rangers' success.

Liam was pleased to see that the age-old adage of practice making perfect was proving to be true. He seemed to get better and better as time went on, and at the finish his touch and shot were so smooth that they seemed almost one movement. Very rarely did he miss the targets by more than a few inches.

After a quick break for lunch, at about 2:00 he once again made his way out to the dirt track around the pitch. At 2:08, after a couple of warmup laps and stretching, he set off.

At 2:37, thanks to a sprinted last lap, Liam was standing with hands on hips, struggling to catch his breath but still with a smile on his face at having beaten his target. He then made his way home, satisfied that he was finally beginning to take his destiny into his own hands, if a little disappointed that it was clearly Lisa's day off.

Thursday was an easy session, and although Liam still found it quite hard, he still coped well with everything he had to do. They finished the session with a little seven-a-side game. The other players were a little surprised to hear

Liam demanding the ball and playing pretty much flat-out. As it was a physically less demanding session, he upped the pace on his run back to the ground and did an extra 20 minutes in the weight room too. He finished with another session on the ball court. He loved his time on the ball court, and really felt like he was striking the ball better and better. He had never known his control to be so on point.

The first team were playing Northwich at home on Saturday. They had drawn away the week before, thanks to a late Ryan McCoughlan goal, his tenth of the season, and this week's game had become very important, as a loss would see Northwich pull away from them at the bottom of the league. At training on Friday, Liam was Robert Regis, Northwich's impressive young forward who just happened to attack the near post on all of Northwich's set pieces...

"You again, eh? Same as the other week, no clever stuff, unless you want to be carried back to the changing rooms, you lairy little runt!" Reggie growled into Liam's ear.

Liam steeled himself. This was going to be a challenge for his new-found attitude and determination. The first free kick was overhit and drifted out of play, although this did not stop Reggie almost ripping Liam's bib clean off him as he grabbed him and pulled him to the ground. The second free kick found its way to Liam, and he got in a quick touch and a good early cross-shot, just before Reggie's right boot took away his standing leg, sending him tumbling to the ground in spectacular fashion. On the side-lines Harry went to take a step forward, unhappy with the challenge, but Alex put his hand across the front of him and motioned for Harry to wait.

The very next free kick found its way to Liam again, this time via a deflection. Despite being slightly sore from the previous challenge, Liam showed impressive reactions to stick out his right foot and control the ball under his studs. He was on the right corner of the area, facing away from the goal towards the corner flag. Reggie was already on the launch pad, ready to fly in at Liam again, but Liam was ready. Reggie took off with a horrible lunge, aiming to make sure Liam got the message once and for all. This, though, was a different player to the one he had previously targeted. Liam caught the ball between his feet and jumped in the air. This left Reggie sliding comically under both him and the ball, in the general direction of the corner flag. Liam then landed and released the ball, before despatching it on the volley straight into his target of the bottom-left-hand corner of the goal - exactly as he had been practicing on the ball court.

An unusual silence came over the training ground for a second, as everyone processed what they'd just seen, then there were a few mickey-taking shouts in Reggie's direction, like "He went that way, Reggie", as well as a few impressed comments sent in Liam's direction. On the side-line, the first-team coaches looked in Pat's direction, wondering just who this young kid was who had made such an audacious play. Meanwhile Alex, standing next to Harry, just winked as he caught Pat's shocked gaze.

For the rest of the practice Reggie was in Liam's ear, telling him just what would happen to him if he tried something like that again. But it was evident to everyone that Reggie had become a lot more wary of Liam and when the ball arrived he wasn't getting too close, not wanting to be embarrassed again. Whatever the case, it did not stop Liam wanting the ball at every opportunity.

Liam ran back to the ground, but he left the weights and only spent a short time on the ball court; he was aware that rest was also important in the lead-up to a game of football, even though he knew he would probably be on the substitute's bench again. He was also very aware that after Saturday he only had four more weeks to prove his worth until the FA Youth Cup quarter-final match against Tottenford, and he wanted to make sure he was ready if an opportunity did present itself.

Chapter Fifteen

Saturday came and Saturday went, as did the next three. Liam was an unused substitute on every one of them. It appeared that Pat had already made up his mind about Liam and was determined to show everyone that he was in charge and it was he who made the decisions.

Despite the unfairness of this, Liam managed to remain surprisingly positive. He was enjoying training, as well as the changes he had seen in himself. He was even finding Mondays and Tuesdays less arduous. He was still doing all his extra work, plus every day in training he was pushing himself to his limits. Rather than being at the back, he was the one now setting the pace. Everyone seemed to be noticing, except the one person that mattered...

Under normal circumstances, Liam would have continued to wait patiently for his chance, but these were not normal circumstances. Today was the last Saturday of his trial period - after today there was the FA Youth Cup against Tottenford and then his trial would be finished. It didn't matter how hard he was working in training, or how much stronger and fitter he was; at the end of the day it all came down to the matches - in football, that was all that ever mattered. So if he didn't get some playing time today, the chances were he never would. He had already decided that he was going to speak to Harry Welch after today's game if there was no change.

Liam had two early setbacks. Firstly, there was no sign of Lisa in reception when he arrived for Johnny's minibus. Secondly, when he got to the training ground and entered the changing room, the first thing he saw was his name next to the number 12 on the team sheet. Jarvis and Neil were again the first-choice front two. Liam gulped down his disappointment. But he was determined not to let either of these setbacks upset him too much, and instead made sure his preparations in the warmup were spot-on. When the game started, he watched intently for any sign of weakness that he could exploit if he was sent into battle.

It was not a good half for Clifton, and at half-time they were losing 2-0. Liam stood in the doorway as Pat spoke to the starting 11 about the first half. He was not happy. At one point he booted the bag of footballs and they bounced off the wall, almost hitting Jarvis. Liam had not seen him like this before. All the players sat staring at the floor, not wanting to make eye contact in case he started on them - a tactic Liam had used before. There was also something funny going on between Pat and Alex. Normally, they shared the team talks. Pat would say something, then pass over to Alex, and they usually seemed to echo each other in their thoughts. Today though, the atmosphere between them was icy.

"Have you got anything to add, Alex?" said Pat at one point. Alex just shrugged his shoulders and looked over Pat's shoulder towards Liam. Pat then looked in Liam's direction for a few seconds as if about to say something, but obviously decided better of it and sent back out the same side for the second half. Alex did not look happy.

Within five minutes though they were 3-0 down, and Liam was begrudgingly sent to warm up. It seemed like he was stretching and jogging for an eternity, and when he was finally called back down to get ready, Liam was chomping at the bit. When he ran onto the pitch there was just over half an hour left. The first ten minutes after coming on, Liam did not get many chances to show what he could do. Clifton were clearly struggling, and as a result they couldn't get any sustained possession of the ball. He did though, through strong running and anticipation, manage to relieve some of the pressure by chasing down clearances and allowing Rangers to gain some unexpected possession.

Then *it* happened.

Jason won another of his trademark towering headers and the ball bounced in Liam's direction, just inside his own half, near the centre spot. Liam was alive to the situation and had already made himself a couple of yards of space through his movement. While on the sidelines, Liam had noticed the away team keeper had a habit of wandering a good ten yards outside his area when he felt the ball was not a threat. But he had not reckoned with Liam.

As the ball bounced, Liam spun and hit the ball on the up in the manner of a goalkeeper taking a drop kick. The next thing everyone saw was panic on the goalkeeper's face, as he realised that he was not where he should be. But it was too late. The ball flew over his outstretched arms, bounced on the six-yard line, hit the underside of the crossbar, bounced back down onto the line, then, almost in slow motion, spun back over the line and into the goal! Liam found himself being mobbed by his teammates as they celebrated a truly remarkable goal.

At this point, a figure in a sheepskin coat and flat cap, who had been watching from the bushes, started to make his way to the number 96 bus stop...

Unfortunately, it was not enough to change the course of the game. In fact, the only thing it did change was the fact that the keeper barely moved past his penalty spot for the rest of the game! Actually, that's not entirely true: there were a couple of other changes. Firstly, in Liam's teammates, who seemed to be feeling a newfound belief in Liam. In truth, this had started in training but now he had produced it in a game, they really felt he had something. They were now actively encouraging him and constantly trying to get the ball in his direction. Also, you could almost see some newfound doubt etched on Pat Waldron's face.

Chapter Sixteen

Liam jogged back after the game. Even after having played only about half an hour, he felt full of pent-up energy and thought this would be a good way to release some of it. He had also started to quite enjoy the run, as it gave him a chance to mull over his day and dissect his performance, thinking about what he had done and how he could improve further. Occasionally, he saw a fellow youth team player stranded on the route, obviously having tried to get one more ring of the bell in Johnny-baiting!

He arrived back at the ground not long after the others. He got his clothes back off Jason and slipped off to the weights room to change. As he went through reception, he saw Lisa dealing with a line of Rangers fans. She was always busy on matchdays, but she still found time to give him a little wave and mouthed "How did it go?".

He gave her the thumbs-up and a smile, then continued to his seat. He had been completely focused on his football over the last few weeks, but it was fair to say that both he and Lisa had tried to find time to *accidentally* bump into each other at every opportunity. There was no doubt that a real friendship was developing.

He was early to his seat, but he liked to watch the players warm up and take the time to read the programme from start to end. He found the match reports for the youth team's last two games and got a thrill from the idea that he could be reading about his goal in the next programme. He also saw the youth team fixtures and that reminded him that he might not even be at the ground for the next home match if things didn't go his way on Tuesday night. The next page was the league table for the first team, and it wasn't good reading. They were third from bottom, with today's opposition just two points ahead of them; this did mean at least that a win today could take them out of the relegation places. It was hard to believe that this was the same club that had won the European Cup about 25 years previously.

As it got closer to kick-off, Jason joined him in the stand, as did Lee Hodges, but the rest of the youth team clearly had better things to do and were probably already spending the money they had got for their tickets. There had been word that there was going to be a protest after the game. He did notice some flags and placards with the words "SALOW OUT" written across them.

Today was another bad day for Rangers. All season under Harry Welch they had been looking more organised, but they lacked quality and were weak defensively. Upfront, Ryan McCoughlan was all about himself. He never ran unless he thought he might get a goal out of it. In addition, he would shoot if he got even the slightest sight of goal, often to the detriment of the team, as teammates in superior positions were ignored.

As for "Chippy" Carpenter, he was so short of confidence it was painful to watch. Time and time again, his ability would get him into dangerous positions, but he would take the safe option rather than taking a risk. An example of this Liam had seen with his own eyes was that at training Chippy would practice free kicks most days, and yet Liam had never seen him take one in a game. Instead, he would just bow down to Ryan McCoughlan and let him take them, even though nine times out of ten he would just end up firing it into the wall.

Rangers took the lead after about twenty minutes, through another Ryan McCoughlan goal. He squeezed it in from an improbable angle, ignoring two teammates in better positions. But twice more afterwards, he chose to shoot in similar positions, and with similar better options. But now the Northwich goalkeeper was alive to it and the chances were lost. Then a nice move from Northwich led to an equaliser, which in turn led to a very nervous last hour for Rangers. They survived wave after wave of Northwich attack, until, almost inevitably, Rangers conceded again. Incredibly though, Rangers snatched their second draw in a week when another hopeful shot from Ryan took a huge deflection to wrongfoot the goalkeeper. The goal, despite its enormous importance, was greeted with near-silence, both out of shock and indifference. A few minutes later, at the final whistle, it was a different story. Resounding boos echoed around the ground, along with chants of "Salow out!". As Liam looked around him, he could see that a large portion of the crowd were now staging a sit-in to protest the chairman's running of the club. In the twisted, irate faces of the fans, Liam could see how deep the discontent ran.

Harry Welch was obviously still popular with the fans though. This was thanks partly to his history with the club, but also, as he had only been in charge for a short amount of time, the fans gave him a pass for the troubles that he had inherited. He even got a modest cheer when he went to the fans to applaud them at the end of the game.

Amazingly, it was only after Liam and Jason had finished their ice-skating clean - two hours after the game had finished - that the noise began to dissipate, as the fans finally began to leave.

As always, Liam made his way back out through reception, secretly wondering if Lisa would still be working. He was startled by a huge eruption of sound. There, on the other side of the glass entrance, were hundreds of Rangers' supporters, banging, kicking and snarling. The venom on their faces shocked Liam for a second, and he looked to his right to see what it was that had sparked such a reaction. Standing there was the chairman, David Salow; he was smoking a huge cigar and was dressed immaculately in a Burberry coat and designer suit. On his face was a look of contempt that he was doing little to hide, and around him were several security guards. The chairman was obviously preparing to make his escape. Liam looked back outside and saw in the background a group of stewards and policemen making their way to the door. Rather him than me thought Liam. A very large Bentley was slowly making its way from the back of the car park, out of view of the ever-growing mob. A few moments later the crowd were forced back, and a gap was made for the chairman to make his way into his waiting car.

What happened next confused, bewildered and shook Liam, as out of the corner of his eye he saw Lisa come out from behind reception. Liam was starting towards her when he suddenly realised that she was making her way to the group that was about to leave. Much to Liam's surprise, Lisa moved to the side of the chairman. Just then, the chairman put his arm around her and they both made their way through the crowd and into the waiting car. As she did so, she caught Liam's eye, then quickly looked away. David Salow endeared himself even less to the crowd by instructing his protecting human guard to "keep that scum off my car," before slamming the door and being taken off, out of the car park, in the direction of Clifton Hill.

As soon as the car had gone, the crowd began to disperse, and the various members of staff went back to their previous posts.

Jason appeared at Liam's shoulder.

"What was that all about, with the chairman and Lisa?" asked Liam.

"What, Lisa Salow? Someone's got to look out for her dad, I suppose." He paused, seeming to consider whether he should continue; he had seen Liam talking to Lisa on many occasions. "Yeah, mate, I keep meaning to talk to you about her. Her dad's a nasty piece of work, and protective as hell. Last year, they reckon one of the YTS lads got released when Salow found out he had been chatting up his daughter and getting a bit too *familiar*."

Reeling inside from what he had been told, Liam thanked Jason for his frankness and bade him goodbye. Jason nodded apologetically and left through the glass doors, leaving Liam alone with his thoughts. Liam felt a sense of betrayal - had she been leading him on all along? What if this was all some big joke to her? A million questions ran through his mind.

Once again, he knew he had to push his emotions back down, and focus on the job in hand. But he also knew that sometime in the near future Little Miss Heiress was going to be a problem that he was going to have to deal with - one way or another...

Chapter Seventeen

Harry was at the end of his tether. Once again it was a Sunday morning, and here he was in his office, high in the stand, mulling over the club's situation and desperately trying to bring in new blood. This was long before any sort of transfer window; in theory, Harry could bring in players whenever he felt he needed to. The problem was his hands were tied. There was no money in the kitty for decent wages and he'd been told that if he wanted to buy then he had to sell first. Which was fine, but one of the reasons he needed to buy was that the squad was paper-thin already. There was a reason they were near the bottom of the league. Who would want to pay top dollar for anyone from a team near the bottom of the Second Division? He stood there at the window, thinking about whether this was the right job for him. He didn't want to be known as the manager who took Clifton Rangers back into the Third Division.

It was then that he noticed Liam - at least he thought it was Liam; he could just about make out that mop of blonde hair. He was running around the dirt track that surrounded the pitch, and what was more, he looked mighty impressive. There was a power and pace to his running that Harry did not remember the last time he had seen him, in the youth team game five and a half weeks earlier. Five and a half weeks ago...

Harry had forgotten all about the deal he made with Pat Waldron. That game must be this week. He picked up a programme from his desk and checked the fixtures. Yes, there it was: Tuesday night against Tottenford. He made a note in his diary and decided that maybe he should get home to Angie. Tuesday was going to be another long day, and coming home earlier than expected today might be the sweetener he was going to need. He knew she would not be happy when he explained that she was going to have another night alone, thanks this time to a lowly youth team game.

Chapter Eighteen

The first two days of the week flew by for Liam as he immersed himself in preparations for Tuesday night. He had begun to see himself as a finely tuned machine and wanted to make sure he was ready and raring to go.

It was a special night for everyone; the FA Youth Cup was a big deal. Successful youth teams often spawned successful first teams, as the winning players made their way through the ranks. The thing was, you only got two opportunities in a career to win the cup: once as a first year YTS, then again in your final year. Rangers were one game away from the semi-final and they were even expecting a few people along to watch.

Liam walked into the changing room and checked out the board. He clenched his fist and said a very quiet "yes," before checking no one had seen him. Then he took his place under the number ten shirt. It still felt special being in the first-team changing room, where so many of his heroes had sat. His trial had flown by. He was hopeful that he would have many more opportunities to sit in this room, but he was acutely aware that it was now down to him.

Pat's team talk was more passionate than normal, as he attempted to get across to the players just what a big game it was. He then went through the set pieces, both defensive and offensive. Next it was onto the warmup with Alex. As they were walking out, Alex put his arm around Liam's shoulder.

"This is it, laddie. Forget all the stuff you've been through. This today is why you're here - this is what you were born to do. Go out there and take this game by the scruff of the neck. There's no pressure, just enjoy yourself. Believe me, this club could do with a Liam Osborne right now!"

When they came together for the stretches, Alex told them how important the FA Youth Cup was, and that winning this trophy could help start a new beginning for the club. Liam could see that Alex's words were wasted on a lot of the other players. The majority of the players were there for individual ambition, but for Liam the words really hit home and just focused him that little bit more. The warmup was completed, then they were in for their final preparations. Liam put on his pads and taped up his socks before slipping on his perfectly cleaned boots, all the while visualising winning the game for Clifton and securing his future. The bell rang, and out they went.

There were about a hundred spectators there, but for Liam it felt like it was a hundred thousand. This stadium had always been special to him, but it was different now. Right now, at this very moment, he knew this was where he was supposed to be.

The whistle blew for the toss, which Rangers lost. Tottenford decided to take the kick-off, and they were underway. It was clear from the very start that it was going to be a tight game. Tottenford were still in the First Division and as such were the favourites. Their play in the first twenty minutes was very controlled; they kept the ball for long periods without ever really threatening the Rangers' goal.

Liam's movement was excellent and the Tottenford defence seemed to sense that he was the danger. So much so that every time he touched the ball, the Tottenford centre-half, an under-17 England international who seemed to model his game on Reggie Stephens, clattered him and sent him tumbling to the ground. Despite this, Liam received no protection from the referee. After 20 minutes Rangers had a throw-in in front of the bench. Liam looked to the bench and saw Alex clench his fist and hold it out in front of him - toughen up. The Tottenford defender, Tony Roberts, was in his ear again, telling him that he was soft and to get used to it - this was only the start.

Liam backed into Roberts, then pushed off him as the ball was thrown to his feet. Roberts's eyes lit up as he approached from behind, ready to clatter Liam again, but, at the last second, Liam completely gave up possession and let the ball bounce through to the oncoming defender. Tony was taken by surprise as the ball arrived at his feet; he was even more surprised when Liam launched into a tackle that took the ball, his legs and all the wind from his body. The Tottenford defender lay there, momentarily stunned by what had just happened. Confused, the referee looked from Liam to Roberts and back to Liam again, before deciding that although he was sure something had just gone on, he could not quite decide what it was.

"Play on."

The ball was still next to the prone defender, so Liam took it in his stride and started to attack the last defender. The defender was caught in a quandary: should he approach Liam, or mark Jarvis, the other Rangers attacker? Liam went to pass the ball to Jarvis, but the defender had anticipated this, and stepped in to take the ball. This was what Liam had wanted. Instead of passing to Jarvis, he passed the ball into the wide-open space behind the Tottenford defence. For a moment, it was not clear why he had done this; there were no other Rangers players in front of him. But it wasn't a pass. Two weeks ago, doing this would have been a waste of time. Not now.

Liam surged forward and reached the ball himself, just outside the Tottenford area. The goalie, who had been caught unawares by Liam's change of pace and direction, belatedly advanced. But it was all too late. Liam side-stepped him with ease before rolling the ball into the now-open goal. The moment of silence again was evidence of the genius that had just been witnessed. Liam stood there, arms aloft, waiting for the rest of the team to catch him up and celebrate.

The rest of the half passed without incident, as if both teams were finding it difficult to live up to what had just taken place.

At half-time there was a definite change in emphasis. Pat's team talk seemed to consist of trying to find as many ways as possible for the other players to get the ball to Liam. This was the final confirmation of his talent that Liam needed. As he went out for the second half, he felt ten feet tall. What followed was an exhibition of pure footballing ability.

In the first ten minutes of the second half, Liam produced two wonderful passes. Most players wouldn't even have seen them, let alone pulled them off. On both occasions Jarvis was alive to the situation, unlike in previous games. From the first pass, Jarvis forced a good save from the goalkeeper, but the second pass ended with a nice side-footed finish from Jarvis to give the Rangers a two-goal lead.

Later in the half, there were a couple of turns by Liam that left the England youth team defender tied in knots. Finally, with five minutes to go, the coup de grace. Twisting this way and that in the crowded penalty area, he finally sent a curling, almost casual shot into the far top corner.

As they started their cooldown, Pat made his way back down the tunnel, only to be confronted by Harry Welch, just as it had happened six weeks ago.

"OK, I know, I know. You were right. He may be the real deal, after all," said Pat, holding out his hands in apology.

"I'm not here to discuss how good he is, Pat. I'm here to tell you to sign him," said Harry.

"That's what I'm saying too. I was wrong - I think we should sign him too."

"No, Pat, you still don't get me. Get your backside back up that tunnel, get him off that pitch and get him signed up this very second!"

"Why the rush?" asked a confused Pat.

"Because, Pat, he just tore to pieces one of the best bloody youth teams in the country, in front of half a dozen scouts, in the biggest youth competition in England. By tomorrow morning my phone is going to be ringing off the hook. We have just showcased one of *the* most talented young players I have *ever* seen, before getting his signature on any kind of contract. I don't care what it takes. By the time he leaves this stadium today, I want his name on a YTS contract, and I want it off in the post to the FA by morning."

Pat had never heard Harry talk like this, and the urgency of his words made him practically run back down the tunnel and to the pitch side, calling for Liam to join him.

It was strange, but Liam felt no nerves as he jogged over towards the tunnel. He knew that he was about to embark on a new chapter in his life. His jog turned into a run. He wanted to start this new chapter as soon as possible...

Chapter Nineteen

So it was that Liam signed his first contract with Clifton Rangers, at the age of seventeen. He would be on £29 a week, although he was told that this would increase to £35 a week in his second year. Little did he know or care that this YTS contract meant he was now committed to Clifton Rangers for the next chunk of his life, as it gave them first option on him when he reached his eighteenth birthday. He happily signed the form there and then, in Johnny's kit room, on top of one of Johnny's old hampers, amongst the sweaty used jock straps. It was not exactly how he had envisaged signing a contract with his home town club would be, but to him it could not have been any more special, and he could not wait to get home and let his mum in on the biggest moment of his life thus far.

Liam ran all the way home despite his aching legs. He sprinted up the stairs and could barely get his keys in the keyhole for his excitement.

"Mum, mum, I did it. I'm a Ranger!"

"Oh, Liam, that's fantastic news! Congratulations, babe," said Liam's mum, grabbing hold of him and giving him a huge hug.

She then sat there as Liam told her every detail of what had happened at the game. She nodded at the right places, and said "Wow" and "That's great" at all the appropriate times too. She knew it was what Liam needed at the time, but she didn't really understand why Liam was exchanging a steady job at the garage for the uncertain lifestyle of a footballer. All she had ever wanted for Liam was a normal life: a steady job, a house, kids - the whole deal. She had spent her whole life protecting Liam, and all of this just sounded far too risky for her liking. But she put on a supportive façade, and so, for Liam, this momentous day had a fitting finish.

The next day was a day off, but Liam was determined not to take his newfound success for granted, and so he continued with his training regime. He was very pleased to increase his record of laps of the pitch to 23 and a half.

He hadn't spoken to Lisa since seeing her with her father after the game against Northwich. This was not easy, as the only way from the ball court to pitch-side was through reception. He didn't even know what he felt about it anymore but to avoid any awkwardness, he ran straight through reception. When he left the ground, he felt surprisingly fresh, so he ran the seemingly short distance home.

Chapter Twenty

As the season progressed, Liam continued getting fitter and stronger and continued to adapt to the demands of his role in the team. It was beginning to become apparent that this season was going to be a pivotal one in the club's history, and that Liam might be about to have a bigger role than even he could have dreamed of.

It was now a rainy Monday night at the beginning of April, the day before the semi-final of the FA Youth Cup. The youth team's season had continued well, largely on the back of some magical attacking play from Liam and some impressive defensive performances from Jason Blackmore. The team had risen up the league and confidence was high.

Unfortunately, the same could not be said of the first team, who, with five games remaining, were still third from bottom. Not good, especially as there would be three teams relegated that season. They would have been completely cast adrift but for the fact that a nasty injury to the Northwich striker Robert Regis had led to a disastrous run for the club. This had meant that the next five games would see either Clifton or Northwich relegated into the Third Division. The problem for Rangers was that, although Northwich could not seem to win a game for love nor money, neither could they! For weeks now it had been as if they were battling each other to see who could gain the least amount of points. It was fortunate for both teams that the two teams immediately below them had been adrift since before Christmas, after record-breakingly awful openings to the season, and, in Bedford City's case, penalties for financial irregularities.

What had amazed Liam was the apparent apathy to the plight of the club shown by some of its players, who still turned up just before training and left immediately after, going through the motions every moment in between. Jason

Blackmore was training with them more and more, as he was now into his last year as a YTS and the club obviously had a big decision to make regarding him and a possible contract offer. According to Jason, who could always be relied upon to be honest, training with the first team was awful; none of the other players spoke to him or passed to him. In fact, they would spend most of the time criticising his every move. This troubled Liam enormously as Jason had been the only one who helped him when he had been going through a similar thing.

Jason would often hold court with the rest of the youth team on the bus in the morning or over a pair of dirty boots, regaling them with tales of the first team's antics. They would all hang on his every word. To some of the team - players like Jason, Liam, Lee Hodges and Jarvis - these stories represented what was wrong with the club, but for many of the others, they showed clearly what they were aspiring to.

"Boys, you should have seen Ryan yesterday! He reeked like a brewery. I swear he was on his phone to the bookies ten minutes before training. I heard Reggie saying that he has been banned from nearly all the pubs in Clifton."

"That's what it's all about, boys!" said Greg Hales, who fancied himself as the youth team's version of Ryan McCoughlan.

Incredibly though, Ryan was still scoring goals and had scored his 22nd goal of the season in the last game, a close loss away to Millham.

These stories always annoyed Liam, who was still a Clifton supporter at heart. It also pushed him to work harder so that he could maybe one day make a difference to what he saw going on around him. This was becoming more and more of a possibility too: every game that he played he got better and better. There were even fans starting to turn up to watch him play in the youth team. Every week there seemed to be more and more scouts as well, coming from further and further afield, all of them keeping a check on his prodigious progress. In the club fanzine, *Bottle of Jameson*, they had even begun to suggest that it was only a matter of time until his first team debut...

The semi-final of the FA Youth Cup was scheduled for the next day against Mansford United. They were expecting a large crowd, as the opposition's first team were currently leading the First Division by seven points.

Harry Welch was looking forward to watching the game, but also knew he had a lot of big decisions on the horizon. The first team were competitive in every game but just could not seem to get over the finish line. What worried him more was the aura of indifference that had seemed to engulf the team. He had tried to address this by bringing in the youth team captain Jason Blackmore. He had an excellent attitude, but even his drive and enthusiasm had been dulled by some of the other players. He also had the difficult decision of when to introduce Liam to the first team, as following some of his recent performances it was increasingly a question of "when" not "if". The reports he had been receiving from his coaching staff were glowing, and there had been interest from other clubs - including tomorrow's opposition in the FA Youth Cup. It was true that they had Liam tied down until he signed his first professional contract, but Harry knew that his chairman's priorities were very different from his own, and he was concerned what the chairman might do if a few pounds were offered for him. It was tempting not to play him until he could sign professionally on his eighteenth birthday. That way, he could get him on a long contract before the chairman became too aware of the possible goldmine he was harbouring. But on the other hand, if they were going to stay in this division, he might need Liam's talent.

Tomorrow was going to be a big day. He had decided that if Liam was as impressive as the reports from his coaching and scouting staff had suggested, then he would have no choice but to put him in the squad for Saturday.

Chapter Twenty-One

"Look, lads, take your time. Take on more fluids, then have a stretch. The game is being delayed for ten minutes as there are more fans than expected. They're opening another section of the ground," said Pat.

At Pat's words several of the boys became visibly paler, the huge significance of the game ahead began to dawn on them. Not Liam though - he seemed to grow in stature at the prospect of such an occasion.

As they stepped out from the cover of the tunnel, it was immediately apparent what had caused the delay. Usually they only opened a small portion of the ground for the youth team cup games, as they only ever got about a hundred or so supporters. With today being such a prestigious game, they had opened a larger section than normal, but even that had proved not to be enough. The stand immediately behind them was partially full, with about one thousand Rangers supporters, but away behind the goal to the left was a sea of red; there must have been more than five thousand Mansford United supporters. They were to find out later that Mansford had put on free coaches to transport their fans to the game. Again, several of the young Rangers players seemed to shrink at the daunting stage in front of them. Liam, on the other hand, puffed out his chest and lengthened his stride, thrilled at the prospect.

Mansford took the kick-off and proceeded to keep the ball for more than 20 passes. The Rangers players were chasing and harrying for all they were worth but could not get near the ball. After the 23rd pass, the ball found itself at the feet of Mansford winger Ryan Wilson. He swayed to the right as if he was about to dribble the ball into the middle of the pitch. The Rangers right-back moved inside in anticipation, but in the blink of an eye Wilson dribbled the ball to the outside instead. He knocked the ball ten yards in front of him, leaving the Rangers right-back tackling thin air. The low curved cross was perfect, as was the finish by the Mansford striker, an Italian. It was 1-0 and no Clifton player had yet touched the ball...

While the Rangers players were standing around like rabbits in the headlights, Liam raced back from his position on the halfway line. He snatched up the ball from the back of the net, ready to resume battle.

"Don't let your heads drop. We still have plenty of time," implored Liam, hoping that this was a good thing.

Liam passed the ball to Jarvis straight from the kick-off – at least he was getting his first touch now. Jarvis then passed it back to the Rangers' 'playboy' central midfielder, Greg Hales, who was put under severe and immediate pressure, forcing him to hoof it blindly forward, straight to the Mansford left-back. The left-back shifted it straight to Wilson, and he was off again in full flight, attacking the now overwhelmed Rangers' right-back Ian Hancock. Without changing pace, Wilson's body shimmied from left to right, not touching the ball. Before he knew it, the Rangers' right back was again beaten and seated on his backside. This time Wilson cut inside and unleashed a fierce right-footed shot into the corner, then went to celebrate in front of the delirious support behind the goal. Rangers were 2-0 down and had only had three touches!

Liam retrieved the ball again, a concentrated look of determination on his face. He got his second touch as he took kick-off again. There were still less than five minutes on the clock. Within three passes Mansford had once again regained possession.

The rest of the half was a pure onslaught, as the gulf between the teams became ever more obvious. In fact, at times, it seemed like it was only bad luck and Jason Blackmore's outstanding effort and anticipation that was keeping the score at 2-0. Every time it looked like Mansford were about to extend their lead, there he was, making last-gasp tackles, clearing headers and blocking shots. It was like the ball was attracted to him, but in reality Jason's reading of the game was exceptional and he often knew what the United attackers were going to do before they did. The post (twice) and the crossbar (once) also came to Rangers' rescue. The half-time whistle was finally blown, bringing some respite for the Clifton defence and midfield, especially Ian Hancock. They were 2-0 down and hadn't had a single shot at goal.

Pat and Alex had a tough job getting some belief into the tired players. A much-needed change followed, with Jarvis sacrificed and another defender brought on to try and limit the damage being done.

Alex then took Liam to one side.

"This is it, laddie, your moment. We've decided we can't throw any bodies forward; they're simply too good for us. That means when we attack, we attack with you, and you alone. We don't want you chasing back - in fact, we don't want you defending at all. We need some magic, laddie, or we're going out." He then looked into Liam's eyes. "You're destined for great things, I'm sure of that, but the truly great players produce on the biggest stages, at the crucial moments. Believe me, laddie, this is one of those moments."

These words were still resounding in Liam's ears as he took to the pitch for the second half. The game started much as the first half had finished, with a last-ditch challenge from Jason preventing another Mansford goal.

Then came the opportunity Liam had been waiting for. The Mansford back four had realised it was the four of them up against one attacker and they were happily playing the ball to each other, eating up the clock as they did so. But Liam had noticed that the left-sided centre-half was very one-footed and on a couple of occasions had taken a risk letting the ball travel across his body when receiving a pass from the left-back to try and get the ball onto his favoured right foot. Liam had been waiting for the perfect moment to pounce.

When the ball next went to the left-back, Liam pulled away towards the right-sided central defender to let him think he had plenty of time. The left-back then played it inside and Liam was off. He approached the central defender from his right side and slightly behind. As the defender moved the ball onto his right foot, he finally noticed Liam, but it was too late. Liam pounced, stealing the ball like a pickpocket snatching a purse. Then he was away, with no one between him and the goal. He made the finish appear easy, as he slipped it low down the side of the goalie.

The funny thing was the celebration: still following their halftime instructions to not venture forward, the Rangers players stayed out of the Mansford area. Liam wasn't wasting any time celebrating anyway. He didn't even break pace, continuing into the goal to retrieve the ball, sprinting back up the field and placing the ball on the centre spot with great purpose. The Mansford players looked confused at this almost theatrical gesture of intent from what they perceived to be a totally inferior opposition, but soon all became clear...

Fifteen minutes later, and after another spell of Mansford dominance, an offside decision gave Rangers' defence some time for recovery. Mansford's defenders did not know what to do. Rangers sent no one forward, and therefore logically Mansford wouldn't have needed to bring back any more defenders. But aware that they still only had a slim lead, they brought back pretty much everyone. The penalty area was packed with red shirts, but no one was really marking anyone, thinking there was safety in numbers. Jason took the free kick, but instead of just launching the ball into the area, he fizzed a ball along the floor in the direction of Liam, who was moving out of the over-defended area, searching for space. The ball arrived at Liam while he was still moving away from the Mansford goal. With his left foot, he flicked it fractionally into the air before hitting the ball with his right foot on the volley. The ball arced and dipped at such an angle that it was never low enough for any defender to block, and the keeper couldn't see the ball because of the defenders blocking his view. Before they knew it, the ball was nestling at the back of the goal. It was an amazing picture: there were no less than seven of their players and not one solitary Rangers player in the Mansford United area, and yet there was the ball sitting in the back of the net.

Once again, Liam raced in to the goal to get the ball. This time, tellingly, he was met with some resistance from the Mansford players. The momentum of the game had clearly changed in their minds, and they were now trying to get some kind of handle on the proceedings. But there, next to Liam, was Jason. He had sprinted forward to help recover the ball, closely followed by two or three Rangers' players. Even Greg was there. They believed now.

The game continued, with neither team now wanting to take a chance and risk losing everything. The referee had checked his watch on a couple of occasions, and it looked like 2-2 was going to be the final score. The ball was cleared deep into the Mansford half, where it came once again to Liam. With no support and surrounded by Mansford players, he tried to get away a quick shot. He shifted the ball to the side and hit it with all the strength he could muster. But the Mansford defence had defended well on this occasion, and as he shifted the ball, two defenders resolutely closed in on him, deflecting the ball harmlessly wide of the goal. They were now well into the final minutes of the game.

Liam took the corner himself. When he looked up, he saw only three Rangers players to aim for. He decided to just whip the ball in under the crossbar and see what happened. But as he struck the ball he slipped, sending it on an unusual trajectory towards the edge of the six-yard box and a barrage of Mansford players. The ball came in at about chest height, moving flatly through the air, seemingly heading into the Mansford keeper's waiting arms. Then, at the last second, a yellow shirt appeared from the crowd of players. With a combination of shoulder and chest, the Rangers player somehow managed to clumsily bundle the ball into the goal. It barely reached the back of the net.

Jason, for it was his torso that had connected with the ball, did not stop running. He kicked the ball further into the back of the net and swung backwards and forwards on the net in front of the stunned Mansford contingent, a primal scream echoing around the whole ground. He was soon joined by the entire Rangers team.

When the final whistle blew, almost immediately after the shell-shocked Mansford United team had kicked off, Harry left the ground, where the Rangers players and supporters were now celebrating. He made his way through the reception and out to his waiting car, having made up his mind on two separate counts...

Chapter Twenty-Two

On the Thursday and Friday the atmosphere at training was highly charged. The whole youth set-up were buzzing with the knowledge of the cup final to come. Those players assured of starting were a little more careful in tackles, trying not to get an injury which would see them miss out, while the players on the fringes of the team trained like it was already a cup final, desperate to be given the chance. Meanwhile Jason and Liam were as ever the perfect role models, training with their usual intensity, despite what lay ahead.

As always, after training had finished, and all the YTS boys had finished their jobs, Pat and Alex entered the youth team hut to give details for the meet for the following day's game. After he had gone through the details for the game - an 8:30 meet as they were away to Brightsea - Pat read out the list of players who were required. A slight murmur then followed, as two notable absences from the squad became clear.

"Liam, Jason, you're at the ground for 12:30…" he said. "See Johnny back at the ground for a first-team tracksuit, and make sure you don't let us down. There are a lot of people counting on you..."

A wide smile spread across his face.

What followed was an avalanche of noise, as the whole youth team, including Alex and Pat, rose as one to congratulate their own. Jason looked sick to his stomach with anxiety, whereas Liam, as was fast becoming the norm, seemed to take the news in his stride. Only the smile from ear to ear gave away that he was feeling any emotion at all.

When everything had calmed down, Pat called the two boys outside to go over what was going to happen, and to give a few pearls of wisdom. "Eat well and rest" seemed the long and the short of it. He also told them not to be overawed and to take in every second of the day. Both boys promised they would and thanked Pat for the pep talk, before returning to the clamour of the hut and then back to the ground. The news had obviously buoyed the other youth team players, as they now had an example of what could be achieved if you worked hard enough at the club.

Johnny was clearly no more impressed with them as first team players than he had been with them as youth team players; with his customary grunt, he threw them two tracksuits and two polo shirts. They then handed him their boots, as one of his pre-match duties was laying out the kit, including the boots, for the first team. Then with a heartfelt handshake, the boys made their own way home, the promise of tomorrow almost too much to take.

Chapter Twenty-Three

As Liam ran over the situation in his mind, he realised how crucial the finish to the season would be. Being a Rangers fan, he knew the first team situation well. They were three points behind Northwich, which meant that their fate was not entirely in their hands. More than anything else, it meant that they needed to start winning some games, although their superior goal difference meant that if they could draw level on points they would likely stay up. He also had another issue to consider. The youth team were in the FA Youth Cup final, and Liam prayed that his promotion would not mean he would have to miss out on it, after having done so much to get them there. His mind quickly returned to the day ahead. He had a nervous excitement that he could not contain, and he hoped to release some of it in the upcoming game.

Things were very different to the match days he had experienced before. For a start, the whole ground seemed alive, even though it was still two hours before kick off. The car park was also pretty full; all the staff who worked in the background to make the match day a success were already in place, busying themselves for the day. As Liam walked into the car park, he was passed by several expensive, clichéd cars, driven by first team players - all Range Rovers and Mercedes. Eager autograph-hunters rushed past him, but the cars didn't slow and not one player even glanced in their direction. Maybe they're too focused on the game, thought Liam hopefully, as he continued towards reception. He was glad that the first person he saw as he entered reception was a friendly face, albeit a very nervous one. He shook Jason's sweaty, trembling hand warmly.

By 12:30, all the first-team players had arrived. As always, Liam was surprised to see that they seemed to have their minds on everything except the crucial 90 minutes ahead. They were on the phone, chasing up tickets, talking about what they were doing that night and a myriad of other insignificant distractions. It was about 1:30 before the players made their way round to the changing room, and even then, it seemed to be a great inconvenience to several of the players. As they did so, Liam saw the Albion coach appear, announcing the arrival of today's opposition.

It was still amazing for Liam to see all these players he had used to pay to watch walking by him as teammates. Chippy had always been his favourite and was still the player that Liam looked up to. He was clearly very talented, but what Liam had noticed was that he was always in the background. Even in training he was always hiding, never quite getting in the right place to receive the ball. When he did get it, he would pass it straight off to the nearest player. Occasionally, when there wasn't a simple pass to play, you would get a quick snippet of his ability. He would seem to effortlessly drift away from his marker before passing the ball off, again to the nearest player. Today was the same thing: he was right at the back, headphones on, hands in pockets, shoulders forward and head down.

Liam could smell Ryan before he saw him. He was frantically chewing gum, but the smell of alcohol was still almost seeping out of his pores. Sometimes it's not good to get a look behind the curtain, thought Liam.

As always, the first thing Liam did when he entered the changing room was check the team sheet. Even though he had expected it, he still felt a tinge of disappointment at seeing his name as one of the three subs. Harry was taking a risk: Jason was also on the bench, meaning that both outfield subs were youth team players. If he had to make a change there was a real lack of experience available.

Doug Clemance ushered the players in, and they soon took their places, waiting for Harry to begin talking. This was clearly a routine they were well versed in.

"Right, settle down everyone, listen up," said Doug, then passed over to Harry.

"Look, as always, we want to get the ball down and pass it - that's why we've got Chippy in there. But, early doors, first ten minutes or so, when it is still a bit frantic, I want us to hit it long." Harry turned to Chippy. "Chippy, once the game slows down a bit and we have more space, we need you to get on the ball as much as possible."

"Sure, boss," said Chippy.

At this point Harry addressed the rest of the team, "I want *everything* to go through him. Understand?"

This was greeted with a few nods. Next it was Ryan.

"Ryan, it's only you up front today, so we need you to be available for the pass to feet. Don't keep trying to run in behind; it's important we can get the ball into you," said Harry.

Liam looked at Ryan and noticed that he barely acknowledged what Harry was saying to him, perhaps trying to avoid him catching a whiff of his breath.

Harry then finished by addressing the whole team again, "Look, we have two young, talented players who are chomping at the bit on the bench today. I won't hesitate to give them their chance, so don't think I won't make changes if need be."

Harry was very business-like and professional in his demeanour as he spoke to the players, and Liam for one was impressed. This was completely the opposite of the attitude that seemed to come off a few of the players. He spoke a lot of sense and Liam felt it was an education to hear the instructions regarding how they were going to play and what they were trying to achieve.

What actually happened was entirely different…

To start with, the Rangers defenders did hit the ball in behind, as instructed. Ten minutes later, the pace of the game had slowed and Chippy started to come to get the ball off the defenders, also as instructed. But, for whatever reason - Chippy wasn't exactly being vociferous in his demands - they continued to ignore him and hit the ball long. Soon, half-time was upon them, and a drab stalemate was all there was to show for the endeavour of the first half.

During the half-time team talk, both Doug and Harry almost burst blood vessels trying to get the players to stick to the game plan. Looking around, Liam was again unsure that everyone was as on board as they needed to be. On a more positive note, he could see himself being introduced to the proceedings sooner rather than later, if things didn't change...

The second half continued much the same as the first, with neither team wanting to take a risk. On the bench, Harry and Doug were going blue in the face shouting for the team to keep the ball and play through Chippy. Their strategy wasn't working. One reason was that in this pressure cooker environment, no one wanted to make a mistake that might cost them dearly, so everyone tried to clear their lines and get the ball into the Albion half as quickly as possible. The other reason was that when Chippy did get the ball, all he could see was the rear of Ryan McLoughlin as he ran away from him, wanting the ball over the top. This meant that Chippy was forced to do the same as everyone else, and just put the ball into the spaces behind the Albion defence. This meant that, for obvious reasons, the rest of the team could not see any advantage in giving it to Chippy. This continued to frustrate Harry and Doug; they had done their homework on Albion and knew that they had a particularly quick defence, so playing the ball over the top was effectively playing to their strengths.

Liam caught on fast and soon realised that Ryan was one of the main issues. If he would just show for the ball to feet, then Chippie would have someone to pass to. Typical Ryan - he was not thinking of the team, just his own gain. He knew that if he showed for feet, then other players would be making runs off him and getting the chances to score. He was not prepared for that to happen. So instead he just kept looking for a pass that was not going to come.

With 65 minutes on the clock, Harry had seen enough and turned to Liam, telling him to get warmed up. Liam launched himself from the bench and practically sprinted down the dirt track towards the corner flag to warm up behind the linesman. This was right by the away support. A barrage of spit and abuse from the Albion contingent made him move a little closer to the dugout but did little to dampen his excitement.

No sooner had he gone than Harry turned to Doug, "We need to do something, Doug; this has got 0-0 written all over it. Maybe the boy can produce that one moment that could swing it our-"

"Hold your horses, Harry," said Doug. "Terry looks like he may have picked up a knock."

Terry Johns was a wily veteran and was highly respected by the other players. He had been one of the first black players to really establish himself in English football, and part of the reason was that he was the size of an ox. Apparently, he had never lifted a weight in his life, nevertheless he was built like a heavyweight boxer. In a game still fraught with racism, Terry had survived, partly because no one had the courage to take him on. If he was limping, there was definitely a problem.

Harry looked towards Terry Johns, their experienced centre-half. Doug was right; he was clearly struggling.

"When are we going to get a break?!" said Harry, "Jason, get warmed up. Send Liam back, be quick. Terry looks like he's done."

With heavy shoulders and to the jeers of the away support, Liam made his way back to the bench. He sat back down and put his tracksuit bottoms back on. He now knew that he was probably not going to get on in this game. With only two changes allowed you couldn't risk throwing on both subs in case you got an injury, so his only chance was just that happening.

"Good luck, Blackie," said a sincere Liam, as Jason stripped off his tracksuit and put his shin pads on. Jason just smiled a nervous smile and took his place at the side of the pitch, waiting for the ball to go out of play.

"Don't muck this up!" snapped Terry at him, as they exchanged places with a token handshake.

The pattern of the game did not change much. If anything, Albion probably had the better of the next twenty minutes. One positive was that Jason was having a very solid start to his debut, making a number of well-timed tackles and interceptions.

Then, with about five minutes to go, Harry turned to Liam and, seemingly on the spur of the moment, told him to get ready - he was going on. The next minute was a blur as Liam prepared himself the best he could, and then he was on, taking the place of the ineffectual Billy Butler. They needed a goal, so he went up front with Ryan.

As he ran onto the playing surface, he was struggling to control the nervous energy in his legs and tripped slightly over a non-existent divot. He jogged awkwardly up to join Ryan.

"Give me the ball. I'll do the rest, kid." said Ryan.

For the next five minutes Liam charged all over the pitch, looking to get involved. Unfortunately, every time he looked for the ball, the Rangers' players ignored his runs and just continued to kick the ball over the top, in the vain hope that the strategy that had not worked over the previous 85 minutes might now start working. Liam was getting more and more frustrated but felt he could not express his frustration as he was still the young player learning his trade amongst these seasoned, experienced professionals.

As he walked off, he was even more dejected to hear the PA give the score of the Northwich game, a 1-0 victory for Northwich. This meant that Rangers were now five points away from safety with just four games to go. A chorus of boos mixed with chants of "Salow out!" rang around the stadium. For a second, Liam's mind drifted at the name Salow. But it was just a second, then the chorus of boos grew to a crescendo, returning him to the present with a bump. He ran the gauntlet, past the overhanging supporters, then down the tunnel and to the sanctuary of the changing rooms.

Back in the changing room, Harry was furious: all that preparation during the week to play a certain way and the second they got out on the pitch it all went up in smoke. His mind was racing as he tried to decide what to do. He wanted to tell them a few home truths, go crazy, throw things, but he realised that nerves and confidence were the problem.

Now more than ever he needed to galvanise the squad and give them the belief they were missing. But how?

He looked around at the players. Did they care enough? He wasn't sure. Some of them looked like they were already over it. His eyes landed on Jason Blackmore - at least he was a plus from today's game. In fact, he seriously wondered if they would have held on for the draw if not for this young man's enthusiasm and athleticism. Next was Ryan. He physically wanted to take him by the throat. He had no doubts about his ability and his goal return this year was very impressive. But when the chips were down, like now, would you really want to go into battle with someone who was only out for themselves? Not to mention his obvious personal problems.

Finally, he looked at Liam. He could see his frustration. In the few minutes he had been on, Liam had made some excellent runs. He had not received the ball when he should have, but his reaction to this was weak. He should have demanded the ball and admonish the players who did not give him it, but he was only 17 and it was a big ask to put so much on his shoulders. He needed more time to grow into himself, but time was running short...

Liam was surprised to see Harry just leave the changing room without saying a word to anyone. Maybe he wanted them to search for the answers themselves, but Liam was not sure his new teammates they had the inclination to do so. Many of them were already joking and laughing and planning their night out. Liam caught Jason's eye and they shared a knowing look.

When they were changed, they both made their way up to the players' lounge. As they stood conspicuously watching the proceedings, the lack of team spirit was evident, as was the huge drinking culture at the club. The players stood in various groups, drinking and laughing - except for Ryan, who sat alone, chasing pints of bitter with various shots. He looked set for the night.

After what they thought was a suitable amount of time, the boys both made their way back down to the foyer of the reception.

"There he is the debutant!" A huge man with a long horse-like face cried out- clearly Jason's dad.

He was with a small group of people who Liam presumed were all Jason's family. One of the ladies in the group gave Jason a big hug.

"Congratulations darling," she said before turning to Liam, "congratulations to you too Liam. You're now a Clifton Rangers first team player! Your mum and dad must be so proud!"

This was a moment for Liam, as he suddenly became aware of what a great milestone in his life this had been. He had dreamed about making his first-team debut his whole life, and yet the combination of a bad result and unfortunate circumstances had meant it had almost passed him by. He hadn't even told his mum about it. He hadn't been sure that she would fully understand the significance of it, but he suddenly deeply regretted his decision.

As he left, some Rangers supporters asked for his autograph and to have their picture taken with the new Rangers player. He felt like he was walking on air as, together with Jason, he made his way out into the car park and started on his way home. But they were to be dragged back down to earth with an almighty, embarrassing bang.

"Oi, where you two going? Changing rooms ain't gonna clean themselves!" came Johnny's unmistakeable growl, much to the amusement of the waiting fans, who had seconds previously been treating them like celebrities.

Chapter Twenty-Four

On Monday morning, a message came from Johnny: Liam and Jason were to report to the gaffer's office. Although they didn't let each other know it, they were both nervous as hell.

When they arrived, they knocked on the door and a voice told them to come in.

"Take a seat," offered Harry, cupping the mouthpiece of the phone to his chest, then dismissing the caller on the other end with a promise to call back.

"Right," said Harry, clearly wanting their full attention. "First the good news: you're both going to be with me for the remainder of the season. Jason, you'll actually be starting tomorrow as Terry is not one hundred percent, although, to be honest, you would have kept your place anyway. Liam, you'll be starting on the bench again."

Both boys mumbled their appreciation but didn't move, sensing from Harry's demeanour that there was still more to come.

"Now to the crux. I'm not happy with the attitude of some of our current squad. If the situation were different, I'd move them on. But I have no choice - I need them, and they know it. We have potential, but I feel we lack focus. I'm telling you this because I want your youthful freshness and enthusiasm in my squad, but I don't want the poor attitudes of some of the senior pros at this club to knock that out of you."

Liam and Jason glanced at each other, shocked and a little uncomfortable about quite how honest Harry was being.

"For this reason, although you'll be with us for all the remaining games, you'll still be training with the youth team. I'll communicate any details for matches through Pat and Alex. But boys, I want you both to remember that

you're in the right with your dedication and attitude –
they're not. So don't let them beat you down; you need to
be examples of the kind of player that this club and I want."

With that, he stood up and walked slowly round to the
front of the desk. He shook hands with both boys, saying
"It's OK, boys. You can smile – you've both got a great
opportunity here."

Both boys made to leave, but Harry motioned to Liam
for him to wait a moment. Liam nodded to Jason, as if to
say he would catch him up.

After Jason had gone out, Harry moved to the door and
held it closed.

Harry said "I just wanted to let you know that you'll get
your opportunity. And, Liam, when you do, make sure you
take it… for my sake as much as yours!"

With that, he opened the door again and moved aside so
that Liam could escape. Liam jogged to catch up with Jason,
and they both made their way back downstairs to re-join
their youth-team friends.

Harry looked out the window at Liam and Jason joining
in with the game of piggy and took a deep breath.

"I hope you know what you're doing, Harry son, I hope
you know what you're doing..."

Chapter Twenty-Five

The next day and a half seemed to last a lifetime for both Liam and Jason. Liam told his mum all about the next game, but although she was immensely proud and pleased for her only child, he could tell that she still did not really get the extent of what was going on. Despite this, he was glad he had shared this moment with her. He knew only too well that lies and deception had played a big part in the house in the past.

The game itself was at their close neighbours Leyton. This meant that it was a relatively late meet. At 6:00, they left their ground on the team bus.

Liam sat staring out the window and thinking about the next game ahead, while most of the team took the chance to set up a card school. Every now and then Liam would glance over, but the amount of money that seemed to be passing hands was almost beyond his comprehension. How could you lose that amount of money and then get off a coach and play to the best of your ability, he wondered incredulously.

After a short while, he started to see quite a lot of Leyton fans. They were going through *their* pre-match rituals, which generally consisted of a few pints in a pub or a full English in a greasy spoon café. Leyton were having a very strong season and had found themselves in and around the pack chasing promotion. This meant tonight's game was equally important for them.

The coach then took a tight, unexpected turn off the main road. Liam was almost shocked at the sight he saw. When he considered how breath-taking the first view of Clifton Park was, it was a shock to see such a ramshackle, unkempt-looking ground. It really brought home how far his home club had fallen when a club like Leyton, who had been in league football for less than five years, were so far ahead of Rangers in both points and ambition.

The coach would not fit in the car park, so they had to park outside the ground, unload the coach and then make their way in through the main entrance. Although a little primitive, the club did have a lovely warm feeling to it. As they made their way through the ground, it was noticeable how friendly and accessible everyone was - a contrast to Rangers. In fact, it was the Leyton chairman himself who met them in the lobby. He showed the team and its entourage to the changing rooms, enthusiastically telling anyone who would listen what a wonderful thing it was to have the mighty Rangers at their humble home. Many of the players sniggered and laughed at the reception they were being given, but Liam felt it gave the club character. He imagined it was the kind of club where you felt a part of the whole and not just a cog in the wheel.

The changing rooms themselves, although clean and well looked-after, were very small and pokey. As a result, Johnny threw them out of the changing room with his normal courtesy, clearly not caring whether it was the first team or youth team he was talking to, so that he could get the kit out and set up the changing room. Liam and Jason wandered out to the pitch to check the surface; it was a chilly night and it seemed like the ground might be too hard for studs. Most of the players just milled around in the tunnel, getting re-acquainted with their phones.

Liam walked out to the centre circle and turned 360 degrees, taking it all in. It was clearly going to be a full house, as every home game this season had been for Leyton. The ground was open, with terracing on three sides and a covered seated stand opposite the dug-outs and changing room. This appeared to be the main area that had been developed since their non-league days. On either side of the ground were two tall sets of floodlights, which were already on, although they did not seem to be too powerful. But to Liam it was all part of the realisation of his boyhood dream; he just prayed that he would now get his much-heralded opportunity, not simply a token five minutes.

The team talk was noticeably different from the last game. Harry focused on the fact that their centre-half had been at Leyton throughout their journey through the leagues, and, although very combative, he lacked pace. The plan was for Ryan to get himself up against him as often as possible and look to try and get in behind for the ball over the top. He stressed, however, that if it wasn't on, they were not just to hit it aimlessly forwards but to play through Chippy as normal. Chippy's face at this point suggested that this approach was not quite as normal as he would like, but he did not say anything. Some of the players raised their eyebrows at the idea of playing through what they saw as a player who was a largely ineffectual luxury. The splits in the team were all too obvious.

Harry purposely had not named the team yet. He wanted to let Jason settle into his surroundings without the other players piling on the pressure. The 12,000 fans tightly crammed into the Leyton ground knew the Rangers team before the majority of the players. But some of them had already guessed from the look on Terry's face that their normal centre-half would not be starting. When Doug ran over the set pieces ten minutes before kick-off, it was confirmed that Jason was starting, and that Terry had recovered enough from his knock at the weekend to feature on the bench with Liam.

The game itself started off very cagily. Tackles flew in from all angles, as both teams vied for the upper hand. It was clearly going to be a very tense evening. Liam watched, fascinated; the atmosphere was electric, and he was looking intently for any weakness he could exploit if called upon. Then, with ten minutes gone, Reggie played a long, driven pass over the Leyton defender Harry had targeted in the team talk. Ryan was in, one-on-one with the goalkeeper. Many players would have panicked, but Ryan had complete belief in his ability. He calmly stroked the ball low to the left of the on-rushing goalkeeper, into the net.

The stadium emptied of sound almost instantaneously. The sound of the small band of Rangers supporters celebrating barely registered compared to the cacophony of sound that had gone before. Then the noise erupted again, as the Leyton fans urged their team onwards. This was in stark contrast with the atmosphere at Clifton Park recently when things had gone against the home team. At this point, shouts towards the bench from the Clifton players let Harry and Doug know that there was a problem with Ryan.

Almost unnoticed by everyone, including the referee, immediately after Ryan had struck the ball, the Leyton defender had clattered into the back of Ryan and left him crumpled on the floor. Harry sent Liam to get warmed up. But Ryan already seemed to have shrugged off the knock and was now back at the halfway line, flexing his leg. Meanwhile, Liam continued to warm up, half-hoping that Ryan was OK and half-hoping he wasn't.

The next time the ball went up to Ryan, the Leyton defender bundled into him, knocking him to the floor once more. This seemed to have the desired effect. Ryan began to move into positions where it was very difficult for the Rangers players to find him. He was clearly not struggling from the knock, but he gave the impression of someone who felt that he had done his job for the day.

Leyton were pressing for the equaliser and providing a lot of evidence as to why they were flying high in the league.

Then came the moment that was to ruin Liam's evening. A clever through ball put the Leyton striker through on goal, much like Ryan had been before. The forward settled himself to apply the finish, when the Rangers centre-half, Lee McGuckin, clattered into him from behind. The Leyton forward had not yet released the ball so the free kick was inevitable, much like the red card that followed.

Now it was Terry's turn to get warmed up quickly so he could take Ryan's place. Rangers were clearly about to enter a backs-to-the-wall situation. They were now playing with no one up front, having decided to keep the numbers in defence where they would need them. Liam's heart sank – partly as a Rangers fan, and partly because, with only two substitutes allowed in a game, the chances of him being introduced were now slim.

This was how it proved. For the rest of the game it was like a training exercise of attack versus defence, with Leyton being the attack and Clifton the defence. To be fair, the Rangers' players were putting in a shift and a half trying to prevent Leyton getting the result they were after. Jason and Terry, in particular, seemed to be everywhere, clearing danger and making last-ditch clearances.

But it was not enough. Leyton ended up taking three of their many chances to run out clear and deserved winners. Once again, Liam was going to have to wait for his chance.

When they got back to the changing rooms at the end of the game, the mood was slightly improved by the news that Northwich had also lost. They had gone down 5-1 at home to league leaders Mansford City, the cross-city rivals of Mansford United.

After the game, Harry was genuinely pleased with the heart his team had shown. He knew that a big plus was the centre-half partnership they had stumbled on. Unfortunately, he was also aware that they were fast running out of time, and with just three games to go, today was another nail in the coffin.

Liam meanwhile, just wondered if he was ever going to get his promised opportunity.

Chapter Twenty-Six

Wednesday was a day off, as was always the case after a game, and training on Thursday and Friday went mostly without incident. Several of the first team did question why Liam and Jason were continuing to train with the youth team, but nothing too much was made of it.

The weekend was going to bring a home game against Petersmouth. The games were running out fast, and once more this felt like a cup final - only a win would be good enough. Petersmouth were a strange team; they played on the South Coast and had a large following, mainly due to there not being much competition for their support locally. They had been in the Second Division for twenty-three consecutive seasons, never really challenging but never really in danger of relegation. What they were was difficult to beat, and so not the best opponents in Clifton's current position.

But this was a game they now had to win.

The team was the same as Tuesday night except for Terry, who was in for the suspended Lee McGuckin. Billy Butler, the first YTS to make it as a professional at the club, came in for Terry on the bench. There was a strange atmosphere at the ground, almost one of resignation, and the estimated crowd would be a new season low for the once-great club.

Harry tried to keep the team talk very upbeat, stressing to the players how important it was they got something from the game. If they didn't and Northwich did, they would be relegated, with two games still left to play. He concentrated on the positives from Tuesday night, praising their work ethic and refusal to give in. By now, tactics were getting less and less significant. Harry knew that at this stage, and in their position, attitude and effort could be all-important.

The game itself was incredibly tight, with very little between the two teams. In fact, Rangers could count themselves very unlucky to go in one goal down at half-time.

At half-time, Harry tried to boost the team up. He implored them to be confident, to get the ball down and pass it. The problem was that the players were too nervous, frightened about going down in history as the one who made the mistake that sent the club down. The news from Northwich wasn't good either: they were leading by a goal to nil at half-time. The thing was, Rangers had to create chances, and the long-ball game was too predictable, especially as the Petersmouth defence were now just playing very deep, protecting their lead and leaving no space to play the ball into. Liam knew that they would need a bit of subtlety and guile if they were to get back in the game.

With 30 minutes still to go, Harry and Doug obviously felt the same, and they sent Liam to get warmed up. Five minutes later, Liam's moment finally came. Doug shouted down the touchline to him to come back to the dugout.

There, he got stripped and ready, while Doug went through the set pieces with him.

"Don't be intimidated; give as good as you get. From them and us," said Doug as Liam stood waiting to come on.

Harry's last words to Liam were "This is your time."

A good early sign as he entered the field of play was that this time his legs did not feel quite so shaky. His chest was pushed out and his chin up. Everything indicated that this time he was truly ready for what was ahead of him.

Once again, Ryan greeted him with the instruction "Hey kid, just get it to me."

"Don't worry about me…" said Liam.

The first couple of times Liam got the ball his touch was excellent, but both times he had few options: Ryan just ran away, looking for the ball over the top again. Knowing that it was not on, Liam just played the simple ball to the nearest Rangers player, much to Ryan's annoyance.

Disappointingly, on both occasions the ball was then just launched forward to no one in particular. Liam had to bite his tongue, but inside he was fuming at the possession wasted after his good work.

The next time he got the ball he faked to pass the ball to a nearby open teammate, but instead he glided past his opponent with consummate ease, then went to put the ball through the legs of his next opponent. It didn't quite work, as the ball got caught between the defender's legs and possession was lost.

"Don't try and be clever," and "Just release it," were just a couple of the criticisms that came Liam's way, while Chippy gave him a knowing smile of empathy. But Liam didn't care. Inside, he knew that he had been unlucky, and that was all that mattered. The next time Rangers got the ball, he went demanding it again.

The game continued, and when the ball next ricocheted in Liam's direction, time was running out. So far, the ball had been arriving at his feet by accident rather than design – it was rather like his experiences on the marshes. Once more, he took the ball easily and smoothly with his first touch, protecting it from the defenders. This time, the defenders were not going to fall for his fake pass and gave him a yard of space in case he tried to repeat the trick. But a yard was all Liam needed.

"Feet!" he screamed at Ryan, passing the ball quickly past his marker.

Ryan had not had time to make the run in behind, so he had no choice but to receive the pass to feet. This clearly took him - and the Petersmouth defence - by surprise.

"Stop it!" demanded Liam confidently, following behind his pass.

Ryan did as he was told, not having the time to react differently to this 17-year old's instructions.

"Leave it. Run!" shouted Liam next.

Again, Ryan did as instructed. He left the ball where it was and then he was off, running towards the goal. The defender marking Ryan did not know what to do - run with

Ryan or try and get to the ball before Liam. In the end he did neither. Liam was quickly onto the ball, and, without pausing, played a perfectly weighted pass into Ryan's path. He had his faults, but the one thing Ryan did better than most was score goals and he did what came naturally to him. His first touch was perfect then he passed the ball into the far corner of the goal with the inside of his foot.

The few fans that had made their pilgrimage to Clifton Park erupted in joy. Even the players who minutes before had been criticising Liam so vehemently, ran to him before going to Ryan to celebrate the goal. They knew he was the one who had crafted it and they recognised how crucial it was.

Meanwhile, Chippy stood there with a wry look on his face, realising that he had been taught a priceless lesson by this boy just out of school.

The rest of the game seemed to fly by, without Liam really getting an opportunity to have any more impact on the game. As the clock ran down, the Rangers players got more and more desperate, knowing that if it stayed the same and Northwich won, they would be going down. Everything they tried failed, desperation making them lack the composure that they needed.

At the final whistle, several of the players slumped to the floor, sure that their fate had been sealed. No one left the pitch - even the Petersmouth players stayed on, all waiting for the Northwich result to come through. They all waited, like a boxer waiting for a points decision. Then it came. First a murmur, then a shout, followed by a huge roar of relief. Northwich had lost, and Rangers would live to fight another day. They were now four points behind their rivals with just two games to go...

Chapter Twenty-Seven

It seemed appropriate to Harry that he was in his office again on a Sunday, looking out his window at the cause of his dilemma, who was running with gusto around the Clifton pitch for what seemed like the hundredth time. It had of course been in this office on a Sunday that he had first heard of this young prodigy, and a Sunday several weeks before when he had been reminded of him again. Now though, he had a huge decision to make, and he was honestly struggling with it. On the one hand, Liam had given a glimpse of the future yesterday, but on the other he understood he had a responsibility and had to make sure that he introduced him wisely. He knew that Liam was still young, and that if he was handled badly, they would never see his full potential. The problem was that there were just two games to go: he might have no choice but to take the risk.

The next game was away to Netfield County, who were already relegated. This was a game that Harry felt that not only could they win, but that they had to win - especially with a home game against league leaders Mansford City as their final fixture. He also knew that before Liam's introduction on Saturday they had been well on their way to yet another loss. Liam's impact had been unquestionable, and in the back of Harry's mind was the nagging question of what might have happened if he had been given more time.

Liam was unaware of the musings going on above him, but he was very aware that he had not played a full game for a couple of weeks now. As well as the first team's final two games, he also had the FA Youth Cup final to come. He had spoken to Alex in training; he was worried that he might not be played since he had not played in the youth team games leading up to it. Alex assured him that he and Jason would be the first names on the team sheet. That was why he was on the pitch, keeping himself suitably prepared.

Mid-thought, Liam checked the clock, and then picked up the pace, conscious he might beat his record if he really pushed on.

Chapter Twenty-Eight

It was one of the biggest games in the club's history, and the preparations could have gone better. Harry's decision to keep Jason and Liam with the youth team made it difficult to go through set pieces and team shape during the week. Harry heard more and more questions being asked from the players as to why they were still training with the youth team, but it was now too late to address. If the first team players knew that their manager thought they were not suitable role players for the younger players at the club, he might have a revolt on his hands - even if it was true.

The other problem was the fact that Netfield was a five-hour coach journey on a good run, and the chairman had cut the expenses budget. This meant they would not be staying in Netfield overnight. A 7:00 a.m. meet followed by a five-hour coach ride was not good preparation for such a huge game, but Harry knew they would need to leave that early just to get the journey out of the players' legs.

The chairman's business had recorded record profits the previous year, but he was immovable and insisted to Harry that they travel on the day. Harry knew that this was totally unprofessional, and it made him wonder if the players' attitude was just a reflection of the club's attitude. It was something else he was going to have to address at some point if the club were to move forward.

Once again, he returned to the Liam situation. He had written out the team sheet on numerous occasions, sometimes with Liam in, and sometimes without. Without meant having an extra midfielder to try and outnumber the opposition in that key area, while with meant a genuine goal threat from Liam and Ryan. There were less than two hours to go before kick-off when the decision was finally made.

Chapter Twenty-Nine

The mood of the players as they arrived at the ground in the early hours of Saturday morning was almost rebellious.

"What the hell is this all about?" said Terry Johns, "In all my years, I've never known anything like it. Biggest game of the season, and here we are meeting in the middle of the bleeding night. Don't they have bloody hotels in Netfield?"

Harry and Doug could hear what was being said, and they were inclined to agree. They had spoken about this and decided to try and use the chairman as a catalyst to bring the squad together.

"Don't blame us; it's the chairman's decision," said Harry.

A few knowing nods went around the rest of the team.

Bill Jameson had always spoken of a siege mentality. He wanted his team to all be together no matter what, with an "us against the world" attitude. This was something that Harry had wanted to build since he had been at the club. Unfortunately, there were several splits in his squad, and there was very little solidarity. In truth, he hadn't helped this with his decision to keep Liam and Jason apart from the squad, something he now knew had been a mistake. Both he and Doug hoped a mutual dislike of the chairman might now bring everyone together.

The journey was quiet, and there was very little conversation. Most of the players seemed to put on headphones and listen to music or fall asleep. Those who didn't set up the usual card school. Once again Liam was shocked to see the amounts being bet. By his reckoning, there were at least two players who had lost more than three thousand pounds during the long journey. Liam could only speculate as to these players' state of mind as they arrived at the ground for the biggest game of their season.

Netfield County were based in the second-largest city in England. In the '70s, both they and the other club in the city, AFC Netfield, were two of the biggest clubs in the country. Despite still being very well supported, they were now in decline and two years ago, they had even started to ground share, something neither team's fanbase was happy about. It was now certain that Netfield County would be joining their rivals in the Third Division next year.

The stadium was still truly magnificent when you saw it from afar, a reminder of bygone years when it used to host the FA Cup semi-finals. But as they made their way through reception, they began to see that it was really a relic. The carpets were worn and faded and there were missing and broken panels in the ceiling. Just like the Netfield sides, it was on the wrong side of its glory years.

The whole Rangers squad were well aware that they might now be looking at their 'ghost of things to come'. If things went badly today, they could be in this position themselves.

There had been very little traffic on the journey, so they had arrived at the stadium with a spare hour before the pre-game ritual was due to begin. Harry decided to take the team on a brisk walk along a nearby canal. Having been cooped up for so long, the players needed a chance to stretch their legs. Their nerves were beginning to kick in, and they walked in near-silence. Liam though felt nothing except the thrill of playing such an important game at such a famous setting. He felt that after his positive influence in the last match he had a real chance of starting the game. His arms and legs were tingling - not from the journey, but at the expectation of what was to come.

The players had just over half an hour to kill after the walk, which did little to ease the nerves. By the time they finally entered the changing room, you could have cut the atmosphere with a knife.

Once again Harry's team talk was delivered with the passion of the true fan; again he dragged Liam with him every step of the way. Liam even sensed that some of the other players were affected by his passion. When he finished speaking, there were several shouts of "C'mon, we can do this!". There was a steely look in many of the players' eyes that Liam had not noticed in the previous games.

The team was announced before they got changed, as there was no longer any need to protect Jason. He had impressed so greatly in the previous two games that it would have been more of a shock if he had not been involved. Liam felt his face drop as he realised he was again going to be starting on the bench, but he forced himself to look indifferent.

Harry explained that he wanted to keep things tight for the first hour and then open up in the last part of the game to try and claim the victory. Although he understood the reasoning, Liam was still bitterly disappointed. He genuinely felt that he would have had something to offer from the start. He did not sulk though; being a Rangers fan, he knew the game was far bigger than the ego of one young player.

As predicted by Harry, there was little space and not many opportunities. The score at half-time was 0-0, and any impartial viewers would have seen it as a poor game between two poor sides. To be fair, Rangers had been extremely strong defensively, with Terry and Jason impressing again. Going forward, they had offered little, although, unusually, Chippy had always been available for the ball. In a clear contrast to previous games he had tried one or two more adventurous things that had nearly come off.

At the half-time team talk Harry just called for more of the same, and so the second half began much the same as the first. After about 50 minutes, with everything going to plan for once, Liam was sent for a long warm-up, and told he was going on in ten minutes. As he warmed up behind the linesman, Liam probably had the best view of the goal of anyone in the stadium. As the cross came in, Liam had seen straight away that the Netfield Country striker had strayed offside. Immediately he shouted for the decision. He then waited for the linesman to signal to the referee, but the linesman did not flag. So it was that when Liam did join the action Rangers were a goal down, chasing a draw rather than the win they had originally sought.

As he took his position, Ryan nodded at him in acknowledgement. Liam nodded back. They both knew the situation they were in.

Liam immediately noticed the difference in Chippy. He seemed to want the ball off everyone, and such was his conviction that more often than not he received it. On the occasions when he did not get it, he let his teammates know that it wasn't good enough - a change long overdue. A confident, more passionate Chippy was good news for Liam. Sometimes Liam had barely started his run when Chippy almost read his mind and instinctively played the ball where he was running to.

For those last 30 minutes Rangers were a real threat. They finally had a way of playing going forward that worked. There was Chippy wanting the ball off the defence and midfield at every opportunity, Liam picking the ball up in the dangerous ground between the Netfield County defence and midfield, while Ryan was constantly on the defenders' shoulders, threatening the space in behind. Netfield were the proverbial rabbit in the headlights: whatever they tried, they were always one step behind. Chippy was the instigator of a lot of the danger, but Liam was at the heart of everything!

When he got the ball, he had options: he could pass the ball back to Chippy then make another run, he could turn and put in Ryan, or, as he did on several occasions, he could take the responsibility himself and run at the heart of the Netfield County defence.

On the first occasion that he took the initiative and tried to take on the Netfield defenders, he lost the ball. Straight away shouts came from his teammates:

"Pass the ball, you flash git."

"Give it easy, you little runt."

"What do you think you're doing?"

They were quickly drowned out by both Liam *and* Chippy telling them where to go! This spurred Liam on even more, and the next time he took the ball on himself, he managed to negotiate his way past two Netfield defenders with a consummate piece of skill, dragging the ball with the soles of both feet. Then, as the third defender came flying in, Liam toe-poked the ball in behind the remaining Netfield County defenders. Ryan was on to it in a flash, and the result was never in doubt. Once again, a Ryan McCoughlan goal had brought Rangers level late in a game. Liam rushed to get the ball from the back of the net, knowing they needed more.

This Rangers side were not finished, and with the referee checking his watch, they won a freekick out wide. They threw bodies forward in one last desperate effort.

Chippy floated in a ball that just cleared the first defender and arrived at about the penalty spot, begging for someone to take advantage. But Ryan was tightly marked, as were Terry and Jason, the other potential dangers.

This was Reggie's 121st game for the club, and in all that time he had barely crossed the halfway line, let alone made his way into the area. On this occasion, he saved himself a telling-off from Harry for not following instructions and staying back, as was his role at attacking freekicks, by launching himself through the air and sending the ball flying into the top corner. He was immediately buried under an avalanche of celebrating Rangers players and a couple of stray Rangers fans. "Stick your bloody hotel where the sun don't shine, Salow!" screamed Reggie from the bottom of the pile with a few of his normal phrases thrown in for good measure!

Netfield barely had time for the stewards to regain order, and to kick off, when the whistle went for the end of the game. The ground was as quiet as a library except for the sound of people leaving and a few die-hard Rangers fans celebrating an unlikely victory. They were celebrating again a few moments later, when the news came through that

Northwich had lost. So with one game left, they were now just one point behind Northwich. The only problem was that the opposition for that last game were Mansford City. Mansford had not been on the best run of late and had lost that day. You would think that would be good news for Rangers, but it meant that they still needed to win to confirm promotion to the First Division and avoid the lottery of the play-offs. This meant the next game was as important to them as it was to Rangers.

The changing room was a sight to see. For the first time there was almost a sense of unity, as the players celebrated a hard-fought and deserved victory. Liam was on Cloud Nine - what a week he had ahead of him. Today, he'd put in his best performance and Rangers had got the three points they desperately needed. Next was the FA Youth Cup final on Tuesday, followed by a game against the league leaders that could seal the club's future. It was almost too much for his young mind to comprehend.

Harry looked around at all the players. Maybe this could be the start of something, things could finally be coming together. He could not help but notice the change in Chippy, and that could only be a good thing, while Liam's performance meant picking the team this week was not going to be as hard as it had been previously.

Before he left the changing rooms, there was one more thing he knew he had to address.

"Great result, lads, but Reggie, you're fined a week's wages, and I want to see you in my office first thing Monday morning!"

The mood suddenly changed, and a hush came over the changing room...

"You were supposed to stay back on attacking freekicks. What the hell were you doing up there?"

The silence continued for a moment, then the beginning of a smile on Harry's face gave the game away and there was a roar of laughter - although Reggie seemed to take a second or two longer than everyone else to laugh, just in case!

Chapter Thirty

Monday brought devastating news for Jason and Liam. "You're first-team players now and this week's preparations are all-important. So, I'm afraid, I've made two decisions, both of which are final. First, you'll be training with us this week; we all need to be together in the build-up. Secondly, I'm afraid you'll not be able to play in the final on Wednesday, as you're both too important to risk injury before Saturday," said Harry.

Both boys took the news like a hammer blow. Their chins hit their chests, and they both felt tears beginning to form. They tried to avoid each other's eyes, as well as Harry's. Liam felt physically sick.

"I understand you're both gutted, but I've no choice. The most important thing is the football club. I also don't want either of you going to the game. It's a distraction you can do without."

The boys left Harry's office and made their way down the stairs without a word passing between them. They had just enough time to tell their youth team friends the bad news before joining the first team for the training session. The youth team players were as distraught at the news as Liam and Jason. They all knew the only reason they were in the final was because of the two of them. Liam and Jason had not been available for the youth team for the last two games, and they had lost both heavily. ·

The week's training was hell for both Jason and Liam, but particularly for Liam. It was like being the new child at school, being picked on by the older, more streetwise kids. Reggie was the ringleader, but he had a little gang of cronies, including Terry and Lee McGuckin, who were more than happy to step in and add their penny's worth. Jason had let Liam know what it was like, but there could have been no preparation for this.

Chippy also came in for some of the same treatment, as they had decided that he had picked his loyalties when he sided with Liam in the previous game. The unity of Saturday had seemingly been forgotten. It was as if the older players felt threatened by the new blood. They were kicked from pillar to post whenever the opportunity arose. If they lost possession trying something different, they were crucified by all of the other players.

Their week wasn't improved by the fact that on the Wednesday the youth team were beaten 5-0 in the final. Neither Liam nor Jason could look any of them in the eye, let alone talk to them. It was a long, lonely week.

By the time Friday came, it was a relief to finally finish training and get a little break. It had been easy in the games to stick up for himself as they were isolated occasions, but the week had drained Liam and he had even found himself doubting his own decisions at times. Chippy had handled it a lot better though. He seemed to have made up his mind that he was going to do what he wanted to do and to hell with what anyone else thought. It was a little harder for a young kid fresh out of youth football to do that, despite Chippy's much-appreciated support.

Chapter Thirty-One

10. Liam Osborne.

Finally, there it was: the last Saturday of the season, and there on the board next to the number ten was his name. Today was the day that he was going to start his first game for Clifton Rangers.

Mansford City had been relegated the season before. Although a huge club in their own right, they had lived in the shadow of their cross-city rivals United for the whole of their existence.

It had been clear from the start of the season that they were going to go all out for promotion. They had bought in Trevor Hurlock as their new manager. He had a reputation for gamesmanship and taking no prisoners, and had made many enemies in his career. He had wasted no time building a team in his image, with a physical edge, alongside a will to do whatever it took to win. His attention to detail was becoming legendary.

Their captain was a young player called Bryan Smith, a former Hod Carrier. His main weapon seemed to be intimidation, both physical and mental, as well as prodigious throw-ins. They also had Morris Dennis, who had been booked more times than any player in the division, and the man-mountain Jimmy Barnett, who had been moved on from every club he had been with but seemed to have found a natural home at City.

They were a physically impressive side who scored many of their goals from set pieces. They had a game plan that they all stuck to, and more importantly they were good at it. They had quite simply overwhelmed and overpowered most of the teams they had played throughout the season. Until recently, that was, when nerves had kicked in at being so close to achieving their goal. Add to that suspensions of some of their key players and they had dropped down to second place and were in real danger of dropping further down, into the play-off positions.

Their preparations were flawless down to the smallest detail: they had stayed overnight in the best hotel in Clifton, had hired out a local sports field for some training the previous day and even brought their own catering team with them.

Liam had seen them arrive. Their coach was owned by the club and was a double decker with ample room for everyone; it even had a sleeping area upstairs.

When they got off the coach there was an air of arrogance about them, none more than Trevor Hurlock. There was quite an entourage with them, carrying bags, equipment and kit - doing the job Johnny usually did by himself for Rangers - but neither Trevor nor the team gave them a second glance. They were totally focused on the task in hand as they entered the reception. But they all seemed to look at Liam as they walked through. This slightly unsettled him, as up to now no opposition side had showed any interest in him. Bryan Smith in particular stared at him and held Liam's gaze for an uncomfortable amount of time...

But now, here he was, sitting in the home changing room, preparing for his full debut. Harry had basically said he wanted the same as the previous game, with Chippy, Liam and Ryan being at the heart of their attacking play. When Harry finished, there were the normal shouts of encouragement from the other players.

Liam took note of Reggie's shout of "C'mon, lads, this is a game for real men today. Let's show some passion." He felt that this was directed at him, Jason and Chippy.

Reggie's pre-game was a sight to see. He would take himself off to the showers, then, clad only in his jock strap, shorts and boots, he would spend ten minutes practising his side-foot block tackles against the wall, screaming profanities as he did so. There were also stories that he had football boots with jagged studs. He would keep them hidden until after the referee had checked everyone's studs, then change into them at the last minute before going out on the pitch. Liam could well believe it.

The ground was as full as it had been for years, due both to the magnitude of the game and Mansford City's huge following. Clifton lost the toss and Mansford immediately spun them around, knowing that Clifton liked to kick towards their own fans in the second half. Liam stood ready to take the kick-off, Bryan Smith facing him. Smith had rolled his shorts right up to the top of his huge quads, and his massive legs glistened with white horse oil. Liam was sure he even heard him growl as he paced up and down like a caged tiger, never once taking his eyes off him.

Ryan passed the ball to Liam, who turned and went to pass the ball back to Reggie at full-back. Then, out of nowhere, came Morris Dennis, sending Liam spinning to the ground. Normally you got away with the first foul, but this was so obvious and reckless that the referee ran over to book Morris, his hand already reaching to his pocket. Immediately, he was surrounded by several City players, getting in his face and telling him that Liam had exaggerated it. Morris got away with just a warning.

Liam glanced to the touchline from his prone position and saw Trevor Hurlock already shouting abuse at the Clifton coaching staff and substitutes. He realised it was going to be a long afternoon.

There were three more heavy challenges in the first five minute: on Chippy, Ryan and then again on Liam. Mansford had obviously planned to take this approach, and even seemed to have divided up who was to make the tackles. These were just the challenges that made contact; every time a Clifton Rangers' player went near the ball, without exception, there would be some sort of threatening approach and challenge from the Mansford City players. There was also a lot of gamesmanship: standing on other players' feet, pinching, spitting and lots of verbal abuse. The Rangers players became more and more rushed, trying to avoid the incoming tackles.

Ironically, the first to be booked was Reggie. He made a fairly innocuous challenge on Jimmy Barnett, but the opposition player proceeded to throw himself to the floor as if he had been scythed in two. The referee was instantly surrounded by Mansford City players and seemed to be almost bullied into producing the card. Just 15 minutes had been played, but the referee was clearly losing control.

The Mansford City team began to get on top. The ball would be transferred quickly from back to front, followed by an aerial challenge that inevitably led to a throw-in, a corner or an opportunity. It was then launched into the area, where it was like the land of the giants. The City players launched themselves in the general direction of the ball, elbows sharp and at the ready. But Clifton Rangers were living a charmed life, and thanks to luck and last-gasp deflections, the ball bounced everywhere but the goal.

As an attacking force Clifton were offering nothing. Chippy looked the most likely to make a difference, with some nice touches, despite the questionable tackles coming in on him. Ryan did not look interested, seemingly keeping away from any potentially dangerous tackles, and Liam was just having one of those games.

No footballer, no matter how great their talents, can perform at their best week in, week out, and for Liam it was just not happening. True, the intimidation and some of the challenges flying in at him were making it very difficult, but he just couldn't seem to get hold of the ball. Even his touch, which was normally so reliable, had deserted him. Several times when he looked to be in a dangerous position the ball just bounced off him, and the away team reclaimed it for another assault. What he didn't need was several of his own team venomously criticising him every time he made a mistake. In fact, it was only Chippy who seemed to offer him any encouragement, despite the fact it was often Chippy's good work he was ruining.

At half-time the score was somehow still 0-0, and as Liam made his way off, Hurlock was waiting for him.

"So you're the great young hope? This is a man's game, son, and you ain't man enough for it. Give up now, you little twat!"

Liam just averted his eyes and kept walking, unable to say a word in response. Hurlock just laughed at him and spat on the floor by his feet. No one saw this except for Liam.

The old doubts began to come flooding back. Was this it, then? Did he really not have the bottle for this? He just wanted to get off the pitch and down the tunnel, then run home, anything but be there.

At half-time, the Rangers changing room was a tough place to be. Both the management and the players knew that they had been completely out-thought, out-battled and out-played. Harry and Doug tried desperately to repair the damage, but you could see that the players were shell-shocked.

The second half seemed to come around all too quickly for the Rangers' players. Once again, the tone was set immediately by a series of uncompromising challenges, followed by yet another barrage of direct attacks on the Rangers goal. More thanks to good fortune than good play, Rangers managed not to concede. When they did manage to get the ball, Liam's lack of form meant that they were offered little relief from the onslaught. It was not all down to Liam's bad play though: he was receiving little support from the officials - or, for that matter, from most of his teammates.

With 20 minutes left, Rangers managed to win their first corner of the game. Liam noticed that City had not put anyone to defend the space at the near post. This was probably due to complacency because of their huge size advantage over their opponents. Liam also knew that Chippy often delivered a low driven corner, so he was sure that if he could time his run right, he could be presented with a good chance to score.

Bryan Smith was marking Liam, grabbing at his shirt and trash-talking. Liam faked to go the far post, then darted back in the other direction as Chippy struck the ball straight towards him.

"Slam!"

Smith's arm extended across Liam's face, the point of his elbow connecting with his cheekbone. Liam went down, holding his face. Smith did the same, trying to make it look like an accidental clash of heads. The incident happened before the ball had got near them, and so the referee could not give anything, as neither he nor his linesman had seen what happened. Liam was taken from the pitch. The Rangers physio, Dave Morgan, used the magic sponge to try and revive him.

Meanwhile on the bench, Trevor Hurlock was goading Harry, telling him that he needed to get his boy off the pitch so the men could get on with the game of football. Glancing across at Liam, Harry couldn't help but worry that he might be right.

Liam did come back on, though he spent the next ten minutes nursing his cheek. Mansford City barely let Rangers have a minute's possession.

Next came the news from the other games. Northwich had taken a 1-0 lead, which meant that even if Rangers were to grab an improbable win, it still would not be enough. Meanwhile, City's other main rival for promotion were drawing, which meant that all City needed was a point. The news had obviously made it down onto the Mansford bench, as Hurlock was now standing at pitch side, screaming at his players to slow things down. He then called over Bryan Smith, and gave him instructions, which were passed onto the rest of their team.

The last ten minutes were painful to watch. Mansford took an age over every free kick, every throw-in and every goal kick. If Rangers did get the ball they were quickly fouled, followed by City taking an age to retreat ten yards. Then there was diving and simulation - the physio of Mansford City must have come on a dozen times in those final ten minutes. Harry, Doug and the Rangers players got more and more frustrated, but the referee had lost control and City got away with everything.

The board went up. Incredibly, there were to be only three minutes of extra time. Hurlock had been in Harry's ear, telling him that he would look for his results in the Third Division next year. He mocked him for playing Liam in such a big game, saying it was desperation. Harry did linger on this point, wondering if he had done the right thing. He was scared that he might have done real damage to Liam's development, and considered taking him off and sparing him any more struggle.

Then the ball arrived at Liam's feet in front of both benches. For once his touch was good, but he was once again sent tumbling to the ground by an awful tackle from behind. As Liam got up and began to slowly limp away, Hurlock snarled in his face.

"Is that it, son? You're done; you ain't up to this. Give me a call when you grow up."

The Mansford City players were all standing around in the faces of the Rangers players, delaying the free kick, attempting to waste even more time. Suddenly, an almighty cheer echoed around the famous old ground. The Clifton supporters were revelling in the news that Northwich had conceded a late goal. For a moment, the City players stopped what they were doing, distracted by the noise.

Chippy, though, was at the ball and staring at Liam. Liam caught his eye and, in a second, he was off running. The Mansford City players were unable to react in time. Chippy lived up to his name, chipping a glorious ball into the path of an onrushing Liam, now clean through on goal.

The Mansford City keeper came charging off his line to close the angle, but Liam calmly slid the ball past him. You could see the Rangers fans, a cheer frozen in their throats, willing the ball over the line. It struck the inside of the post and, unfortunately for Liam, spun along the goal line before being scrambled away for a corner by the recovering City defenders. Liam held his head in his hands.

"You might as well sod off home now, cos it's not your day!" said Bryan in Liam's face as he marked him from the corner.

At that, something inside Liam stirred and built up inside him. As Chippy was beginning his run-up to take the corner, he turned to face his tormenter.

"This *is* my home!"

And Liam propelled his head into Bryan's stunned face. Smith crumpled to the ground, and Liam accelerated into the space at the near post. Chippy's delivery was flat and driven as usual, but it arrived to Liam at an awkward position, at knee-height while he was still facing the corner-taker. Liam jumped in the air. It was as if he was going to allow the ball to travel through his legs, but then whipped his left heel backwards, catching the ball perfectly. The ball was in the net before any Mansford player could react. A stunned silence followed, as was becoming usual after moments of Liam artistry. Then the crowd erupted.

The City players surrounded the referee in protest, but to no avail, as again neither he nor his linesmen had seen the incident. Liam was off towards the dugout to celebrate with Harry. This was the goal that could keep Rangers in the Second Division. As he approached the Rangers bench, he slid on his knees, facing the livid Trevor Hurlock. When his slide stopped, he was only yards from where Hurlock was standing. Hurlock saw Liam raise his hand to his ear and give the universal "phone me" gesture at him before being buried below a sea of celebrating Rangers players. This meant that Liam did not see the Mansford City manager being held back by several members of the management team.

Mansford City just had enough time to kick off before the final whistle went. Harry moved towards the City bench for the customary handshake, but Hurlock brushed past him, ignoring his extended hand and marching up the tunnel.

"Good luck in the play-offs!" Harry called after him having also heard the other results of the day.

He then turned to his players. They had begun to make their way off the pitch, but he sent them back on to thank the fans for their support. For this group of players, this had been their first taste of what a glory day at Clifton Park was really like. He hoped it would instil a hunger for more of the same...

Chapter Thirty-Two

Officially, Saturday was the last working day of the season for the Rangers' players, but they still needed to come in the next Monday to clear out their stuff, get weighed, have any injuries checked out and to do one or two bits of press work. There would usually be an end-of-season 'do', but due to how disappointing the season had been, the club had thought it prudent to cancel it several weeks previously.

After Liam's match-winning, season-saving goal, he had been called in for a bit of press work for the club. He had received mixed reviews of his "head butt". Many members of the press who were present felt it was accidental, and even several of those that felt it was on purpose had laid much of the blame on the lack of protection he had received from the referee. This was before TV cameras were at every game so whatever the truth was, there would be no trial by TV. No retrospective ban would be forthcoming.

He took the lift up to the fourth floor, where the press room was situated. He was not expecting what he encountered there. Walking through the door marked "Press Office", he was caught off-guard by the sight of a waiting Lisa Salow. She looked just as uncomfortable as he did.

It was the first time he had seen her since watching her get in the car with her dad, the chairman. She momentarily took his breath away. He had forgotten the effect she had on him. She mouthed hello, but he acted like he had not noticed. She was standing with a large balding man and the club photographer. The balding man welcomed Liam and invited him to sit down.

"Hi Liam. I'm Stuart Richards, the club press manager, and this is my assistant, Lisa." He gestured in her direction, clearly not aware of their history. Liam did not even look at her. "If we can just ask a few questions about how things have gone since you joined the club and get a few pictures for the fanzine."

Liam took a seat and they began to talk, while Lisa took notes. A few times Lisa tried to catch Liam's eye and offer a smile, but he was resolute in his efforts to ignore her. They took some pictures, then thanked Liam for his time, and off he went, like a sprinter out the blocks.

He was halfway back down the corridor when he was stopped in his tracks by an indignant voice calling his name. He spun on the spot to see a red-faced Lisa marching towards him.

"What was that all about?" she said. "You barely acknowledged I existed in there!"

It had clearly upset her.

Liam looked long and hard at her before replying. "I thought the likes of you would be far too important to talk to the likes of me." He had not known he was going to say that.

"What's that supposed to mean? I've never been anything but nice to you. I actually thought we were friends"

"Friends? Friends trust each other. I trusted you, but it was only one-way. You're the chairman's daughter! You didn't think that was something I should know? Or am I not *important* enough?"

Even Liam was surprised by the venom in his voice. He knew he was probably overreacting but he had shared things with Lisa that he had never shared before while she had kept secrets. There had already been too many secrets in his life. When he saw the hurt on Lisa's face there was a moment that he wished he could take it back. Then his pride got the better of him, and he stormed off towards the lift.

Lisa just stood there, stunned at his outburst. She knew she should have told Liam who she was, but she also knew she did not deserve this. She wanted to run after him again, but her own pride stopped her. The truth was that seeing him today had stirred up old feelings in her. This was not the ending she had envisaged or hoped for.

Liam stood facing the back wall of the lift. He did not even press the button to go anywhere. His heart wanted him to go back and make things right between them, but he was too stubborn. Besides, he felt that he might now have gone too far for there to be any reconciliation. He had waited for this moment for what seemed like forever, and had never been sure what he would do. Now he was not entirely sure that he had done, or said, the right thing. He leaned forward and rested his head on the cold glass of the lift, trying to clear his head and get his thoughts straight - it felt like they were spinning out of his control. He slowly reached forward and pressed the button to take him back down to reception, and was surprised to find himself fighting back tears yet again.

As he did so, Lisa was wiping her eyes and solemnly making her way back to the press office.

Chapter Thirty-Three

After that, Liam avoided entering the building anywhere near the offices. He spent the off-season keeping up his fitness regime, ready for his first pre-season. He had heard the players talking of pre-season with dread, and, as it was to be his first, he wanted to make sure he got a head-start on it. He continued to go to the ball court every day, and his touch and striking of the ball continued to get better and better.

Liam had noticed that he never won any 50-50 headers; all the defenders towered above him. This meant that he was reliant on other players to make good passes to him, and so there were sections of games that passed him by. He was determined to improve his spring when jumping.

He hung a balloon on a piece of string in the rafters of the upstairs gym, and every day he would attempt five hundred headers on the balloon. Each day he managed to reach it he would raise it slightly. By the time the rest of the squad were back from their holidays for the start of pre-season, his jump was reaching Michael Jordan-esque levels.

There were not many changes from the previous season. Money was still an issue. The club had released two squad players to make space in the budget for Liam, and for Jason Blackmore, who had signed a one-year contract. Reggie was also given another year thanks to his performances at the close of the previous season. Harry had hoped to bring in one or two players, but in the end he did not have the resources to do so. This meant that going into the new season they were once again among the favourites for relegation.

Nothing could have quite prepared Liam for his first pre-season. For the first two weeks Liam only saw a football when cleaning boots in the hut. That in itself was proving to be a chore of epic proportions; Liam had been given Terry's boots to clean. Terry saw this as an opportunity to exert power over him, and when he was in front of his little clique he would look for any chance to ridicule and chastise Liam for the job he was doing.

"Oi, boot boy! You missed a bit!"

"Sorry Terry."

"That's no help, just because you think you are a big-time Charlie, doesn't mean you are any better than the other YTS boys. Now get them clean!" With that, Terry hurled the boats towards Liam much to the amusement of his little gang.

Liam picked up the boots and started to make his way back to the huts to clean them again. As he walked, he looked at the boots. It was true there was a dirty mark across both boots. Liam knew it hadn't been there when he put the boots out for Terry that morning. He knew better than to argue with Terry.

It also didn't help that Liam's first pre-season came during a very hot summer. He used to spend half the sessions waiting for clouds to drift across the sun.

"You OK, Liam?" said Doug after what was a particularly tough session.

"I just feel a little dizzy. I'll be ok."

"Best not take any risks. Get yourself down to the medical room and see the doc."

The club doctor was a funny man. He wore a bow tie and a tweed jacket, and you could see the blood vessels on his nose – he was clearly someone who enjoyed a drink. He had a reputation for giving out tablets like sweets, as well as being quick and easy with an injection. He made a good additional income from the club, and therefore was quite happy to do as he was asked, not wanting to rock the boat. He knew his job was to get the players back on the pitch as soon as possible.

There was no drug-testing programme to speak of, which was a good job, as none of the players took any responsibility for what they were taking. Liam could remember when he first joined the club he had got a knock on his troublesome knee during a game, and being sceptical when given a couple of anti-inflammatories to take that night. The first-team goalkeeper, Jimmy Mimms, had openly laughed at him, telling him of the veritable smorgasbord of tablets he had lined up on his mantelpiece, left over from various hand-outs.

Despite finding pre-season incredibly hard, Liam acquitted himself well. All the players from the youth team and the first team went for a run each day through the local woods up and down the hills. The players were set off in different intervals, with the slowest starting first and the quickest setting off last. The idea was that everyone would finish practically together, ready to start the next activity. Each player was also timed and had to beat their previous times. The run always seemed never-ending. On the first day Liam and Jason were sent off in the middle, but by the third day they were both running in the final group.

They were also weighed on every Monday, which some of the players clearly dreaded. Several of the players were known to have a sauna before arriving at training on a Monday, and many of them ran with black sacks under their shirts to sweat out the excesses of the weekend. During the pre-season, Ryan always gave the impression that he would rather be anywhere than at the club. He also seemed to have many small niggly injuries that, suspiciously, kept him from doing some of the harder sessions. When he did join in, he put in so little effort that he might as well have been in a random bar, or in the bed he had clearly just stumbled from. He even cheated on the run through the woods, hiding amongst the trees until the players came round for the second lap, then joining in again.

The pre-season games went well for the club, with Liam, Chippy, and – unbelievably - Ryan looking dangerous when Rangers were in possession. Terry and Jason looked very solid in defence, and Reggie's obvious passion and desire gave some bite to the team.

Unfortunately, Reggie was still on Liam's case. If anything, he had been worse since they had returned to training, as both of the players released to make way for Jason and Liam had been part of his little group. He lambasted Chippy and Liam at every opportunity. The thing was, it was very difficult to just ignore it, and at times both of them made bad decisions through trying to avoid his wrath. It wasn't just his wrath either - he still had several allies in the first team: Terry, Lee McGuckin, Jimmy Rose and Malcolm Minton. That meant three of the back four and two of the starting midfield were constantly on Liam, Jason and Chippy's backs. It was the same in training, where every opportunity was taken to belittle them.

They had just won their third pre-season game and were back in training. They were still doing long runs, and as usual Liam was getting stick for being out in front and "sucking up". All the normal things: "Slow down", "take it easy", "settle yourself down."

Liam had had enough. He thought back to their conversation with Harry when he and Jason were first brought into the squad. About how they were the ones in the right, not the senior players. Liam decided to make a change from within. When they said to slow down, he ran faster, shaming the players who could not keep up. When they started playing a game in training, he dribbled past Terry and got in a shot.

"Oi, runt, take it easy!" said Terry.

The very next time Liam got the ball, he popped it through Terry's legs, making him look even more foolish. Terry was fuming and spent the rest of the session trying to get his revenge. Liam didn't care; he just kept getting on the ball and playing his own game.

He didn't stop giving his all until Doug called for a finish to the session. Even when the other first team players started trooping back in, he stayed out, practising finishing into the empty goal. He was ashamed by their attitudes and had been since he'd arrived at the club. He was not there to make friends. This was his dream, and he was not going to let it slip through his fingers because of some lazy, apathetic players going through the motions. All this did not go unnoticed, either by the unhappy senior players or by the impressed coaching staff.

By the time Liam started making his way back to the changing room, all the first team had gone and the car park was empty. He gave Jason his clothes, so he could take them on the bus back to the ground. They were drenched; one of the clique had clearly thought it would be funny to throw them in the shower. Unlike when the YTS boys had messed with his clothes Liam didn't even bat an eye. He was happy that he was getting to them. Jason said he'd see if he could sneak them into one of Johnny's army of tumble dryers. Liam then started on his run back.

As he ran, he thought over his actions that day. He was convinced he had done the right thing, and readied himself for the inevitable comeback, resolute that he would not relent - no, that he *could* not relent.

The next day was more of the same. If anything, Liam became even more ruthless, looking for chances to make Reggie and the rest look bad. Doug wanted to intervene but Harry stopped him; he felt that there had to be changes. And so the pattern continued day after day.

By the time the pre-season games had finished, and the first official game of the new season had come about, there was a definite and obvious split in the team. On one side were Reggie and his cronies, and on the were other were Liam, Jason, Chippy and Billy Butler, as well as Scott Fulling, another young player who played at right wing for the first team.

After five games, Rangers found themselves in the bottom half having drawn four and won just one.

For Harry and Doug, it was incredibly frustrating. While there had been a huge improvement from the previous season, they sensed that if they all started pulling in the same direction, they could be set for a very exciting season. On top of it all, the next game was at home to Mansford City. In the play-off final, City had been beaten on penalties, having never fully recovered from the game at Clifton Park, but they had started this season running and were sitting on top of the table with five wins out of five.

Chapter Thirty-Four

"Remember me?" spat Bryan Smith as he smashed into Liam from his blind side.

Liam picked himself up. Bit his lip. Said nothing. This time he was going to let his football do the talking. Word of Rangers' improved performances had spread, and crowds at Clifton Park were up. This meant there were about 7,000 Rangers fans screaming at the referee to do something every time Smith smashed into Liam. But like in the previous game, the referee seemed intimidated by Mansford City's approach and let play continue.

The difference was that Liam was now on top of his game. Although he was on the wrong end of a battering, he still looked capable of opening City up at any moment. Every time a Rangers player got the ball, there he was, demanding it off them. His legs were black and blue, and blood tickled down his shin, but he still went on demanding the ball and trying to play his own game.

Early on, Reggie and his group had almost enjoyed seeing the treatment Bryan and the other Mansford players were giving out to Liam, but even they had stopped taking pleasure in it. More and more, Liam resembled a beaten boxer refusing to stay on the mat.

The crowd winced as yet again Liam was cut in half by an outrageous tackle - this time from Morris Dennis. Even the referee could not ignore this one and flashed the yellow card in a sneering Morris's direction. As Liam began to rise to his feet, Reggie helped him up.

"Take it easy, kid. It's a long season," he said.

"What do you care? You don't even know what side you're on," said Liam, through gritted teeth.

He then shrugged Reggie off, immediately demanding the ball off Jason from the free kick and looking to take Dennis on again. This time, he beat him, before playing a nice pass into Chippy. Chippy returned the pass to Liam, and he again looked to take on a City player, but was taken out by a badly timed - or possibly well-timed - slide tackle from a Mansford City defender.

Liam rose heavily to his feet, looking physically worn out and barely able to support his own weight. Ryan stepped up to take the free kick, ignoring the waiting Chippy. Liam was just about to say something when Chippy grabbed the ball off Ryan and pushed him out the way.

"I've got this," he said, with such certainty that Ryan didn't even bother to argue. Clearly Liam's attitude was having the desired effect.

Chippy stood over the ball and backed up. He was about 25 yards out and to the right of the goal. He strode up and bent it majestically round the wall into the top right corner. It was never in doubt, and it was thanks in no small part to all his extra practice after training. The whole Rangers team celebrated in front of the Clifton faithful. Everyone except Reggie, who stood on the halfway line contemplating what was happening around him, and Ryan, who was slowly jogging back for kick-off, seemingly oblivious to the whole thing.

There were still 15 minutes left when Mansford kicked off. For the next ten minutes they put the Rangers goal under extreme pressure with their now-familiar aerial onslaught. Then a far post cross was headed clear by Terry, into the path of Liam, who was tight to the touchline. He killed it instantly, then, out of nowhere, came Smith. He launched himself two-footed around Liam's calves, sending him spiralling into the barrier.

Bryan was quickly on his feet. He was standing above Liam's prone body, snarling expletives, when he was knocked to the floor by a lunging Reggie. Within seconds, all the players were there, pushing, shoving and threatening – well, all but one; Ryan stood uninterested on the halfway line, hands on hips.

When the referee was finally able to separate everyone, he sent off Bryan, as well as Reggie, who was still in Smith's face.

"What's your problem, Reg? You don't even like him."

"He's a Ranger, Smiffy - just like me. That's all you need to know!" replied Reggie as they were both led off down the tunnel.

Liam and Chippy exchanged a confused look. Neither of them fully understood the significance of what had just happened...

The game finished as a 1-0 victory for Rangers, with Liam removed from the battlefield for his own protection shortly after the red cards.

Harry, as wily as ever, didn't miss a thing. He wondered if this was the moment he had been waiting for. Maybe their season was finally about to start...

Chapter Thirty-Five

On Monday, training seemed to be following a familiar pattern. The players were doing a box-to-box running drill. They started on the goal line, then sprinted to the six-yard box and back, then the edge of the area and back, and then every other line and back, finishing with a long sprint from one end to the other, then the same in reverse. As usual Liam began to pull away from the other players, and as usual one of the clique - Lee McGuckin on this occasion - began to give him some stick, telling him to stop making them look bad. Liam just told him to stop whingeing and to work harder - then he wouldn't look bad. Just as Lee was about to bite back, he was interrupted by an unlikely source.

"He's right. Shut up and work harder," said Reggie, digging in deep and beginning to give pursuit to Liam, who was by now well out in the lead.

Lee did not know what to do, except follow Reggie's example. Liam had heard what Reggie said, and he slowed for a second to glance back at him.

"Don't slow down now, runt!" said Reggie, winking at a shocked-looking Liam, then overtaking him. Liam responded by starting to chase him down.

***

The next few weeks were exciting times for Clifton, as they steadily rose through the league. By the middle of November, they were firmly in the play-off positions. They were the most in-form team in the league. Other than Ryan, there was a togetherness to the team now, and Reggie had become Liam's unofficial enforcer. Everyone in the league soon knew that if you took liberties with Liam, within minutes you would be on the wrong end of an equaliser from Reggie. The whole team were like a single unit, and they all knew their roles and responsibilities and stuck to them.

Liam was key. He didn't score a lot of goals, but those he did score or assist on seemed to come at key moments: winning goals or late equalisers. In fact, at the end of November he was voted the division's young player of the month, and even Reggie's old clique seemed genuinely pleased by this.

But then there was Ryan. Most days he turned up for training still the worse for wear. During games he was only interested in personal glory; he never did his defensive duties and rarely looked to play in his teammates. Even though his goal tally was already in double figures, thanks to some wonderful approach play from Chippy and Liam, he barely even celebrated his own goals, let alone anyone else's.

Harry knew he was going to have to do something about the Ryan situation, but he had something else on his mind. Liam's 18th birthday was on 29th November. This meant he would now be eligible for a professional contract. Harry had an appointment to see the chairman to find out exactly what they were going to offer him. He hoped the meeting would go without a hitch.

Chapter Thirty-Six

"Mr Salow will see you now, Mr Welch," said the chairman's over-worked and under-valued personal assistant, opening the door for Harry.

"About time," thought Harry, whose four o'clock meeting was now a 6:15 meeting - as if he didn't already have enough to do!

"Take a seat," said Mr Salow, offering a chair but no apology. "What can I do for you?"

Harry sat down, resting his hands on his knees. He wanted to act as relaxed as possible, so as not to let the chairman realise what a big moment this actually was.

"It's about Liam Osborne, the youth team player we have playing for our first team at the moment. It's his 18th birthday next Thursday, and I think we should offer him professional forms," said Harry, attempting to be casual about it.

"Ah, yes, I know the lad. I'm going to sell him to Mansford United," the chairman replied, dropping the bombshell in equally casual tones.

"W-what did you say?"

"Yes, I had a phone call from Mansford United and they are prepared to pay £100,000 for the boy. That is clearly very good business for a 17-year-old who has only played a handful of games, and who we came by for no fee. This will look very good in the company ledger."

"But, Mr Chairman," began Harry, clearly flustered. "You can't... think of the club... the town..."

At this point a marked and unnerving change came over Mr Salow.

"The club! The town!" he bellowed. "Mr Welch, my whole life has been devoted to this club and this two-bit town. My father worked himself to an early grave to bring success to this club, and what thanks did he get? None. Do you know, as a child and a young man I barely saw my own father because of this bloody poisoned chalice of a club. We nearly lost our home on numerous occasions, as he threw away our personal fortune for *this club*. Even when my poor mother was ill and her body so frail that she couldn't even lift herself out of bed, he still never missed a game. As for me - huh! He would remember Martin Richards' birthday before mine. You would think I was the black sheep of the family, just because I didn't follow his passion for football. All over nothing but a game, a bloody game! Well, no more - not me, Mr Welch. This club is a business, not a hobby, and I will never, *never* let sentimentality cloud my judgement!"

Harry sat back, taken by surprise at this glimpse into the chairman's psyche. He knew he had to think quick. The next few minutes would be crucial if the season and the club's future weren't to disappear.

"Of course, sir, I fully understand what you are saying, but you misunderstand me. Yes, right now, £100,000 is a good price for this lad - a good piece of business as you say - but if you hang onto him, if you give him a long contract and bide your time, he *will* be worth *millions...*" Harry left the last word hanging in the air.

Mr Salow stood up, his interest now clearly piqued. "Millions? Really? For a 17-year-old? How can that be possibly be?"

"Well, you see," started Harry. "Right now he can see out his contract and then walk away from us for nothing. This means anyone who wants to buy him is completely in the driving seat - that's why United are trying to get in early with such a *small* bid. But if we put him on a four, or even better a five-year contract, then anyone who wanted to buy him would have to pay serious money. In two or three years, given the right support, he could make you rich, sir."

The chairman turned to face the wall behind his desk, deep in thought. Harry waited on tenterhooks, praying his fast thinking had saved the day.

"I am already rich, Mr Welch, but what you are saying does make business sense. Offer him a four-year contract, but try and keep the wages down, with no signing-on fee. To my mind, he has already cost me £100,000, so as an asset he has made a loss. Make sure my initial outlay is kept under control," he finally said, all business.

Harry stood up for a handshake, but none was offered, so he took his leave, a relieved man.

Chapter Thirty-Seven

Liam's love for Clifton Rangers was definitely taken advantage of during the talks over his contract. The final word from the chairman sent down from on high was that Harry should offer him five years, not four, obviously thinking this would make him more valuable.

Liam was offered terms of just £150 per week for a regular starter in a side near the top of the Second Division. This left a bad taste in Harry's mouth, but his hands were tied. What he did do, though, was put in a few bonuses that he knew the chairman would not take seriously when he checked over the contract. These bonuses were for achievements that seemed unrealistic at that moment in time, but if any of them were to materialise, then Liam would be extremely well-compensated for his loyalty, much at the chairman's expense...

Liam signed the contract before the game against Hullingborough on the Saturday. For the first time in his life Liam truly felt like a man, especially when he saw the look of pride on his mother's face as she stood at his side on the centre spot, in front of a hugely appreciative and noticeably large crowd. This was to be the first time she had seen him play live at Clifton Park.

Liam had an outstanding game, seemingly inspired by his future being sealed, as well as the attendance of his mother. Rangers battered Hullingborough from the start to the finish. The winning margin would have been far wider but for Ryan shooting from every conceivable angle, shooting even when it was obviously not a realistic option. He did still get his customary goal though, when Liam burst through the Hullingborough backline, drew the keeper out of his goal, and then squared it for Ryan to finish. Most players would have celebrated with Liam following his unselfish approach play, but Ryan barely celebrated at all.

It was noticeable that the rest of the team ran to congratulate Liam and ignored Ryan altogether. Looking on, Harry realised that things had gone too far.

After the game, Liam met his mum in the reception, and took her up to the players' lounge. She could not have been prouder, positively beaming the whole time. Until she saw Ryan, that was.

He was sitting alone, a blank, empty look on his face. There were already several empty glasses in front of him, and he was attacking his latest drink like it was the last in the Western world.

"That man," said Liam's mum, an anguished look on her face. "The one who you helped score. Liam, look at him, can't you see? You of all people... that isn't right, he needs help. I, I can't..." Her face became ashen. "He reminds me of..."

Then she was off, apologising to Liam over her shoulder. She made her way out the door of the players' lounge and was away down the stairs. Liam looked after her, and then at Ryan. He understood what she was hinting at, but didn't know what to do. He followed her out the door.

Harry watched all this happen from the back of the room. He decided that, come Monday, he had to have some kind of plan. But at that moment he had nothing.

Chapter Thirty-Eight

At training, Harry stood next to Doug as they watched the players doing their warmup. They couldn't help but notice Ryan. He was a mess. He had his customary black sack on and he was sweating profusely. All the other players were joking and laughing as they jogged, but Ryan was alone, several yards off the pace.

"Look at him!" said Harry in an exasperated tone. "I'm going to have to pull him after training!"

"Leave it alone, Harry. There's more to this than you know. That's a can of worms you're looking to open there," said Doug.

Harry looked at his friend and colleague. He trusted Doug implicitly, and he obviously knew something that Harry didn't. He had intended to try and tackle Ryan that very morning, but had a feeling that it might be a good idea to probe his friend on the subject first.

When they finished their warmup, they started a basic passing drill. Harry saw how the squad was pushing themselves, making every pass and movement count. The most impressive was always Liam. His passes were crisper, his movement was smoother, and he dragged everyone with him, pushing them to their limits. Everyone, that was, except Ryan, who appeared to be going through the motions once more, just getting through another day...

Harry called him over. He could smell the alcohol immediately, seeping through his pores.

"I don't get it, big guy. You've got so much to offer, and you must see we're going places, but you're still just going through the motions. You need to get on board, or you won't have a future here."

Ryan slowly turned to meet Harry's eyes. "Do what you have to, boss. I've got 11 goals already this year. Someone will want me - my bills will still get paid, whether I'm here or somewhere else."

Harry was astounded at the matter-of-fact way he delivered the words. He felt like screaming at him but when he looked deeply into Ryan what he saw was a broken man. Ryan just raised his shoulder in a non-committal, flippant gesture and walked off to join the rest of the players.

Harry turned to Doug. He had a "told you so" look on his face.

"I may need to have a bit of a chat with you after training," he said. "The Royal Oak? I'm buying"

Doug just smiled. He was never one to turn down a free drink.

Chapter Thirty-Nine

Harry put the two pints of Guiness down on the table and pulled up a chair.

"Go on then. I'm all ears"

It transpired that Doug had been behind Ryan coming to the club on a free transfer three years previously. They had been in the First Division together at Whitecombe, where Doug was training the reserves. Doug had got the offer to be number two at Rangers so decided it was time to step up, while Ryan had finally worn out the club's patience and they had been desperate to move him on. Doug had thought a change of scene might do Ryan some good, even though Whitecombe was only about twenty miles away. Unfortunately, he had brought his demons with him.

Harry listened intently.

"OK, I get all that, but you said there was more to it. None of what you've said is particularly news to me."

"I was coming to that. You see Ryan wasn't *always* like this. When I first joined Whitecombe, he was the golden boy. He still scored goals for fun, but he was a team player... and a family man"

"A family man? But I never knew-"

"Exactly, it was a rough breakup," said Doug. "He's got two young 'uns too - positively doted on them, he did. They were always an explosive couple. He's always liked a drink, but you know football, it was no more or less than anyone else and she was the same. They were always out on the town together; the local press loved them. Then came the kids, and she changed, naturally, but he didn't. It's hard to tell now whether the drinking started the rows, or the rows brought on the drinking, but he spiralled out of control. In the end she had no choice. She threw him out, but that just made him worse. He pulled away from everyone, family and friends included. He's been on a downward spiral ever since."

Doug paused and took a long swig of his drink.

"The drink's his problem, but she's his issue. I don't think he's even seen his kids, or her, in the three years since he came here. Inside he's dead, Harry. I thought coming here would be the answer, but to be honest I think it's all too late for him."

They stayed for a couple more drinks, discussing various club issues. Harry then got a couple more details off Doug, and they went their separate ways.

In the pub car park, Harry made a call to directory enquiries. Then, after several brief telephone conversations that cost him the best part of 60p, he set off on an impromptu 20-mile journey.

Chapter Forty

Harry pulled up outside the house. He was shocked by how lovely and well-kept it was. He knew that Ryan lived in a run-down apartment in the town, often returning there staggering and the worse for wear. But this was a detached house in a small, picturesque village just outside Whitecombe, and was clearly worth a lot of money.

He knocked on the door, and was greeted by an attractive but tired-looking woman in her late twenties or early thirties. She opened the door and introduced herself as Mary McCoughlan. After exchanging pleasantries, she invited him in. As they walked through the hallway, Liam saw various toys littering the floor.

"Sorry for the mess. Darren and Sarah are upstairs, but they seem to leave a bit of themselves wherever they go!" She laughed and her face changed; she looked suddenly more carefree. "You were very candid on the phone. Is there a problem with Ryan? Every time I get a call about him, a part of me waits in *dread*."

They both sat down.

"No, no, it's nothing like that. I'm concerned, that much is true, but I feel a little out of my depth with regards to Ryan and I wondered if you could help."

"He has that effect, Mr Welch. I spent four years out of my depth, trying to raise a family with a man who wouldn't grow up, wouldn't accept his responsibilities. Do you know what it's like watching the man you love self-destruct, and being unable to do anything except make matters worse?" The words poured out of her, her anguish was still clearly apparent.

Harry noticed that she spoke in the present tense. Mary seemed to sense what Harry was thinking.

"I won't lie, Mr Welch: I hate the man he's become, but he's still my husband and the father of my children, and I don't think I'll ever be over him."

Harry was taken aback. He chose his next words very carefully.

"What if we were able to work something out, get Ryan back on the straight and narrow... where would you be in that new life, if at all?"

Mary rose from her seat.

"I've told you already, Mr Welch, he's my husband. I hate the man he's become, but I will always love the man inside, the man I married." She held up her left hand, a wedding ring still on her finger. "I would move heaven and earth to get *that* man back. I never gave up on him; he gave up on us. I know the story is that I threw him out. It's not true. He just stopped coming home." Her voice broke slightly and a tear slowly made its way down her cheek.

"I'm glad you said that, Mrs McCoughlan, because I don't think what I have planned would work without you..."

Chapter Forty-One

Saturday's game was away against Louth, a four-hour coach trip away. Once again, they had to travel down on the day, but unlike before, there was no moaning about this. Ironically, the chairman's indifference towards the team had brought them closer by giving them some common ground: their mutual dislike of the chairman. The siege mentality that Harry had been looking for was now firmly in place.

The game itself was a hugely important one: a win could see them in the automatic promotion places, and the whole team was buzzing on the journey down, with one notable exception. Ryan sat alone in the middle of the coach, staring blankly out of the window. There was still a card school, but Harry had set a limit of £200. If you lost any more than that, you were out of the game until next time. It made Liam laugh: £200 was still more than he earned in a week! But it was better that they all arrived focused on the game, and not concerned with whether they could pay their bills that week.

Louth was a harsh northern market town, and the ground sat amongst a myriad of factories, their towering chimneys spewing black smoke. When the game kicked off, there was no smoke coming from the chimneys; they had clearly closed to allow the workers to support their local team. It was a great atmosphere and a very tight game. In truth, it could have gone either way as the home crowd inspired Louth to an excellent performance, but in the end class told and a trademark Chippy free kick decided the game.

When the team returned to the changing room, Johnny's ancient transistor radio informed them that they were now up to second, just five points behind Mansford City. The atmosphere in the changing room was electric, and on the way home they stopped for a fish and chip supper courtesy of Harry, and a couple of crates of beer courtesy of a few of the senior players. Harry noticed that Ryan had brought himself a large bottle of cheap whiskey for the journey home.

All the players were grouped at the back of the coach waiting for the order from the chippie to arrive. They were drinking, singing and doing what footballers do - taking the mickey out of each other! In this setting, even the most personal and outrageous comment could be brushed of as banter - there wasn't an "ism" that was considered taboo. The team spirit was there for all to see. It was a stark change from the splits that used to run through the core of the team.

There were two exceptions: Liam joined in with the general mood but did not touch a drop of beer, and Ryan sat alone drinking himself to a stupor.

Harry decided now was the time, before they continued on their journey. He made his way down the aisle.

"Not joining the lads?" he asked innocently.

There was no response from Ryan.

"Oh, that's right. I forgot: you're Ryan McLoughlan, you don't care about anything!"

Still no response.

"You just sit there then. Wallow in your own self-pity, tell yourself how the world has done you wrong," goaded Harry.

There was still no response, although Ryan had turned his head slightly towards Harry, clearly listening to what was being said.

"The great Ryan McCoughlan doesn't want anyone, and no one wants him. Traipsing his path alone, sod everyone else, incapable of forming a relationship with anyone or anything. What is it that you're trying to prove?"

"What would you know?" said Ryan finally, still with no real emotion.

"Oh, I know plenty... I know you walked out on a wife and kids, I know you care enough to live in squalor so they can live comfortably. I also know you love a bottle of Scotch-" At this point Harry pushed the half-full bottle of whiskey in Ryan's hand, making it clink on the glass of the window. "More than your own flesh and blood."

At the last comment, Ryan swung wildly at Harry, but only connected with the headrest of the chair next to him. The conversations and banter suddenly stopped.

"There he is, *finally*. He has a heart, and there is something he cares about - not that he cares enough to do anything about it."

"What do you know? How can you talk about my life? Walk a mile in my shoes, then see. I had everything, and I threw it all away. Do you think I want to be like this?" He held up the half-full bottle. "Do you think I don't want my old life back? Well I can't - it's too late. She doesn't want me, and the kids don't even know me!" He was shouting now and the rest of the coach had fallen into an awkward silence. "Three years since I last saw any of them, and there's no going back for me."

"What a crock! Is that what you've told yourself? You just aren't man enough to do anything about it." Ryan tried to respond, but Harry cut him off with a gesture like a policeman directing traffic. "You have people who still care for you. I'm one - and you know what? Mary's another!"

The very mention of her name clearly stung Ryan to his core.

"That's right. I've seen her," said Harry. "And you know what? She hasn't given up on you either, in fact as far as I can see, the only person who has done that is you. So you can sit there with your bottle, reminiscing about what could have been, or you can do something about it. You know, a good man - and a great manager - once told me that it's always darkest before the dawn. You know what? Right now, you are at your darkest point. As far as I can see, there's only one way to go. When you wake up tomorrow in that hole you call a home, with a stinging head again, have a good long look in the mirror, then take your first step! You know how to reach me."

With that, and without glancing back, he moved back down the coach and took his seat at the front, next to a concerned-looking Doug.

The rest of the journey was very subdued, the memory of their victory fading into the past. Ryan sat there and finished his bottle of whiskey before passing out. Then, as had become a regular occurrence, Terry and Reggie practically carried him home, Ryan's arms slung limply over their shoulders.

Chapter Forty-Two

On Monday morning at 7:00, before any other players had arrived at training, there was a knock on Harry's door and a dishevelled, beaten-looking Ryan walked in.

"I need help."

Chapter Forty-Three

The money to check Ryan into The Priory came from the players and Harry. The players all chipped in a substantial percentage of their wages, and Harry funded the remainder from his personal savings. As a result of this overwhelming generosity and support, two weeks before Christmas, Ryan was checked in for a six-week stay. The Priory was an addiction treatment centre, hidden away in a secluded area of Southgate, North London. It had become very popular amongst the troubled rich and famous since its opening in 1986. It was not cheap but had a very notable success rate.

He was allowed no visitors for the first seven days and was to later say it was the hardest week of his life. But he stuck at it and fought harder than anyone thought possible; the nurses proclaimed they had never treated someone with such drive before. Ryan knew why he was doing it, and it spurred him to complete commitment. After the first week, he was allowed to nominate two visitors, who could come for 30 minutes each day - these were normally family members.

The first visitor was Harry Welch, the other signed the signing book simply with the name "Mary". Club commitments meant Harry had no choice but to miss several visits, especially over the hectic Christmas period, but Mary never missed a day, including Christmas Day itself.

Without their main goal threat, Rangers' season stuttered slightly. They still managed to pick up their fair share of points, but they dropped out of the automatic promotion zone and back into the play-off places. This period of the season would have been a complete disaster if not for the growing influence of Liam. He had never felt much of a need to score, even going back to his days of playing with Nigel Walters on the marshes, but he knew that now they were without Ryan, he had to step up. He seemed to lift the whole club on his back in this period, revelling in the extra responsibility.

In the 12 games that Ryan missed, Liam scored ten goals - including two with his head, thanks to his balloon on a string. He gave away no less than seven bottles of champagne to grateful teammates, all won for being man of the match. At the end of January he became the first player in Second Division history to win both Player of the Month and Young Player of the Month simultaneously.

But Harry knew that he needed Ryan back. There was no way Liam could continue at this level without some kind of burn-out.

When Ryan did return to the club at the start of February, the club were hanging onto third place. By the time he had regained full fitness and worked his way back into the first team, they were down to fourth but still well in the race.

The change in Ryan was substantial and clear. When he returned to training, he worked as hard, if not harder, than any other player at the club - even Liam. By the time he got his starting place back, he was fitter, lighter and quicker than he had been during his whole time at the club. For Liam it was a godsend. With a player that quick, even an average pass looked good, and Liam's passes were never less than good. He seemed to be able to put Ryan in behind opponent's defences almost at will, and with computer-like precision. In his second game back, Ryan scored his 12th goal of the season, followed immediately by his 13th.

That though was not the story of the game. The true momentum-changer was when Ryan was put through in the last few minutes to complete his hat-trick. Ryan surprised everyone by rolling it square to Liam, his unmarked strike partner. After the game, Liam admitted he had nearly missed the open goal that Ryan had presented him with, but he was able to scuff it in off the post to put Rangers 3-1 up and finish the game off. As surprising as the pass was, the look of delight on Ryan's face, as he rushed to congratulate Liam on the goal was even more surprising.

The whole team celebrated in front of their travelling support. Even Jimmy Mimms left his goal and sprinted the full length of the pitch to join in. Harry knew that his team was now going to take some beating.

So it was to prove, as Rangers went on a ten-game winning streak that took them back into the automatic promotion spaces, with Ryan scoring an impressive twelve goals. This was not the only significant series of events to hit the club during this time.

Liam had just finished in the ball court one Thursday afternoon when he spotted Lisa leaving the main building. He quickly ducked back into the shadows, wanting to avoid another unwelcome confrontation. Before he knew it, a silver Hyundai had pulled up and Billy Butler had got out. Billy walked up to Lisa and kissed her on the cheek, then she took her place in the passenger's seat and they drove off.

This was the second time in his short Clifton career that seeing this beautiful young lady get in a car had stirred deep emotions, emotions that he felt he had no control over. But on this occasion, he knew exactly what he was feeling: it was jealousy. He knew he had no right to feel it, but it swept over him like a terrible, all-consuming cloud. It was ten minutes before he was able to pull himself together enough to leave the shadows and make his way home.

Chapter Forty-Four

The ten-match winning streak that followed Ryan's return to the team meant that as the season reached its final month, Clifton and Mansford City were overwhelming favourites for promotion. By a strange twist of fate, the two of them were once again scheduled to meet on the final day of the season. But before that, there was even more drama to come.

Liam saw Lisa with Billy on many occasions after his discovery of their 'friendship'. The word at the club was that they were seeing each other and it was a serious relationship. What made it worse for Liam was the fact that Billy was such a likeable character. He had been one of the first of the first team to accept him, and he felt an affinity with him as he had also come through the YTS scheme, just as Liam had.

Despite Liam's discomfort, life continued at the club as usual. But one morning at the training ground, Liam was walking up to the house to get ready for training when he saw Billy coming in the other direction, boots in hand.

"Hiya Bill," said Liam jovially.

Billy glanced up. His face was red and his eyes puffy. Liam went to say something, but words escaped him. Billy sped on, head down, and Liam continued on his way, bemused.

Throughout training, Billy was the sole topic of conversation. News spreads quickly at a football club, and before long a picture had emerged of what had happened.

Apparently, the chairman had visited Harry at home the previous night, raging about the rumour that Billy had been seeing his daughter. Harry had not taken it too seriously at first, but this had just enraged the chairman even further. The long and the short of it was that the chairman wanted Billy out, and he wanted him out now. Harry had no choice about it, so that very morning, he had told Billy that his contract would not be renewed at the end of the season and that he was to be put on the free transfer list. Not only that, he was being put on extended gardening leave until the end of the season, having broken the club rule against fraternisation with staff.

A few of the players spoke about going on strike, but they were empty words: they all knew where the power lay. Plus, they were on the edge of promotion to the First Division and every one of them had far too much to lose. Most agreed with Terry, who said that all they could do was make sure they got promoted then Salow would have to pay Billy the big fat bonus that would come with it. Needless to say, the name Salow was not a popular one that day. Liam largely kept quiet, thinking about Lisa.

Chapter Forty-Five

The remaining games went to form, and the penultimate match soon arrived. They were at home to their local rivals Leyton. A draw would give them automatic promotion to the First Division and the whole town was yellow and blue again.

A full house was predicted for today's game - the first in nearly ten years. Older supporters likened what Harry was doing to the revolution brought about by Bill Jameson all those years previously.

Liam could tell it was going to be a special day. When he arrived at the ground for the 1:30 meet, there were already about 50 fans waiting at the entrance to get players' autographs. As always, he signed everything put in front of him with a welcoming smile and happily posed for pictures. It was all still a little surreal to him. When he finally entered the stadium, he felt a longing to go and speak with Lisa, to share this special day with her in some way. But he didn't.

The team that took to the field that Tuesday night were already tired. Out of the entire league, Clifton had by far the least players in their squad. Most weeks it had been the same eleven who took the field. The club had only used fifteen players all season – the lowest number of any team in the league by far. There was a potential 16th on the bench for that match: Greg Hales had been brought in from the youth team. Having Liam and Jason as role models had clearly had an effect on him; he had earned his place through hard work and dedication - the Clifton Rangers way.

The game itself flew by, and the Clifton fans did not stop singing once. Forgetting their tired limbs and inspired by the occasion, the Rangers' players put in a prodigious shift and rewarded their loyal fans with a sumptuous performance. Fittingly, it was Ryan who scored the two Rangers' goals that not only confirmed their promotion to the First Division but also pretty much confirmed that he would win the Golden Boot as the league's top scorer - despite having missed two months of the season.

As the final whistle blew, the party began. It seemed like everyone from the club found their way onto the pitch, from the laundry lady to Sue, the training ground cook. Lisa would have loved to have joined in the celebrations, but given what had happened with Billy Butler she didn't want to put a dampener on the proceedings. Looking out over the festivities, her eyes immediately fell on Liam. She had genuine feelings for him and was longing to tell him how proud of him she was. But she didn't.

Chapter Forty-Six

It was a strange twist of fate that paired Mansford and Clifton, the two teams that had already gained promotion, for the final game of the season. Most experts agreed that the First Division would be a better place for having them, with both clubs having impressive histories and young, ambitious managers at the helm. City were 3 points clear of Rangers and with a far better goal difference so had already been all but confirmed as champions.

The large Mansford City squad had allowed them to carry out a good deal of rotation, meaning their players could rest and recuperate. By contrast, Jason and Liam had played an incredible number of games for a couple of raw teenagers in their first full season of senior football, featuring in every match. Ryan had been through the mill as his body adapted to its new life, and he was not the only player who clearly needed a good post-season rest.

Harry's team talk was celebratory: he congratulated each and every player, going round the room shaking hands and recalling some moment in the season where they had truly played their part. When he'd spoken to the final player, he stood in the middle of the room and took a deep breath.

"Every one of you has helped to add a new chapter to the esteemed history of this great club. Today isn't the culmination of all our work, just another step along the road. To quote the greatest leader of men I have ever known: 'This is not the end. It is not even the beginning of the end. But it is, perhaps, the end of the beginning." At this, a few players exchanged glances and sniggers. Harry's quoting of Bill Jameson, who had in turn borrowed a lot from a certain Winston Churchill, had been getting more and more frequent. "With that in mind I am making a few changes today," he said, and was met by some intrigued expressions.

Harry then went on to select a team minus Jason, Liam and Ryan.

"Well done, boys. You have all more than played your part, but right now we start preparing for next season, and this game would be one game too many for you. We need you to be ready to fight another day. As for the rest of you, we still have a game to win - do me proud!"

The three of them were clearly not happy about missing the game, but there was not a player in the room who didn't know deep down it was the right thing to do. As the three of them took their place on the bench, still in their team tracksuits, Trevor Hurlock called across to them, accusing them of not fancying it. But they just smiled knowingly back, then spent the next 90 minutes cheering on their team.

The game itself was a non-event as a spectacle. Both teams knew that the job had been done, and they simply went through the motions, one eye on the battles and celebrations still to come. The 0-0 scoreline was a fair reflection of the contest.

The atmosphere in the ground was like a carnival, as both sets of supporters came together in celebrating their glorious successes. At the final whistle the whole stadium stood to salute both teams, and as the Second Division trophy was presented to Bryan Smith and the Mansford City team, even the Rangers supporters clapped their fiercest rivals.

All that was left was the customary handshake between the two managers. Harry held out his hand, half-expecting to be rebuffed again, but instead Hurlock shook it warmly. Releasing his grip, he set off to celebrate with his team, but then turned back, "Oy, Harry," Harry turned, curious to see what Hurlock had to say. "See you next year!" he called with a wry smile and a wink.

Chapter Forty-Seven

The players all put their bonus for promotion together, then split it down the middle and sent half the total to Billy. It was a show of support and a defiant gesture to the chairman, who had refused to give him any kind of severance package. This also meant the whole Billy and Lisa issue was still very much in the players' minds.

Unlike the previous season, this year the club had a great deal to celebrate, and the end-of-season party was going ahead. As is traditional at this kind of thing, all the members of staff were invited, from ticket sellers to cleaners. The hospitality suite was full to the brim and everyone was in high spirits. There was one cat amongst the pigeons, though.

Lisa had decided she wasn't going to go, but her friends in the press room persuaded her otherwise, particularly as for her it was a double occasion. Stuart Richards in particular considered her a good friend. He knew more about her circumstances than most and was very insistent that she *had* to go. Lisa had at first been adamant that she wouldn't, but Stuart's badgering did the trick, and she reluctantly agreed to meet him there. Besides, she still felt she had unfinished business.

She knew the stories that had been doing the rounds, portraying her as a spoilt brat playing with people's lives. She knew the truth, but had promised Billy that she would keep his secret. She just wanted the night to pass without incident.

Of course, Liam spotted her immediately. Like Lisa, he just wanted the night to be over with. On the football pitch he was confidence personified, but off the pitch he was still a nervous, insecure teenager. All night he didn't know what to do with himself. There was a lot of backslapping and congratulating going on, and he managed to always keep a lot of people between him and Lisa. But he had to fight the urge to go and talk to her, which got stronger and stronger as the night went on.

The other players were drinking the night away, and he could hear them sniping about her. They still saw her as the main reason that Billy had been released from the club.

As well as Liam, there was one other player not drinking a drop: Ryan. Despite this, he still seemed merrier than everyone else put together and spent the night with a huge smile on his face. This was partly because he had been dry for nearly five months, but mainly because standing next to him all night with a matching fixed grin was Mary. They had not reconciled completely, but for the last few weeks he had been spending a couple of nights a week at the family home. Even though they were in separate beds, those had been the happiest nights that Ryan could remember. He felt like he was walking on air. Harry kept looking over at the two of them and smiling, both inside and outside.

About midnight a lot of the older members of staff began to leave, as did those who had families. The younger staff members started making plans for alcohol-fuelled nights out. At this point Lisa plucked up enough courage to approach Liam one final time.

She made her way across the room towards where he was standing.

"Sod off, princess," said Terry, who was standing by Liam.

"Yeah, why you even here? Has Daddy sent you?" said Lee McGuckin, blocking her way.

"Out the way. It's Liam I want to talk to, not you," said Lisa, struggling to hide the tremor in her voice.

"Well, he don't want to talk to you," said Terry.

She felt trapped by her emotions. She knew that if she said another word, she would break down. Unable to escape, she turned to Liam in desperation, looking for some sort of support. Liam caught her gaze. He wanted to say something, seeing her in such obvious distress tore him to his heart. He went to speak, to tell them to leave her alone, to tell her his true feelings, but no words came. The silence and distance between them was painful for him, and for her it was too much. She dropped her drink, sending glass and wine across the floor. She mouthed a swallowed "thanks" to Liam, and then turned and ran for the door, desperate not to let them see her cry. Not to let *him* see her cry. Let them think they had won. Let *him* know that she cared.

While all this had been going on, Stuart had been watching from the bar. He had deeply hoped that someone would step in on her behalf, praying for Liam to step up. When no one did, a surge of fury came over him. He started to make his way over to the source of his anger.

"Just look at you lot, there in your ivory towers. Don't worry about actually knowing the facts!" he said, trembling with anger.

"Ivory tower! That's rich! We all know who lives in an ivory tower, funded by her father!" Terry replied.

Stuart looked up at Terry. He was an intimidating sight as always, but Stuart gulped down his misgivings and continued.

"Yeah, well done. Once again you're talking about something you know nothing about. Her father cut her off the moment she started working for this club. He didn't want her anywhere near this place. But she loves Rangers - something she got from her granddad. You know, the man who helped put this club and this town on the map. He used to take her to games when she was a kid.

"She has worked her backside off at this club. She's here despite her father, not because of him. She's been living in a tiny little flat above the chemist's in the high street, with not a penny coming in from him!" He took a breath. "As for Billy, that's between him and her, but they were never more than friends. She had a blazing argument with her father over the whole sorry affair and she hasn't spoken to him since. That's why she's moving away!"

"She's moving away?" Liam said, a little too quickly, stepping in front of Lee and Terry.

"Yeah, the Billy incident was the final straw. She's taken a place on a media course in Netfield. Tonight is her last night - not that you care!"

Liam didn't hear the last words; he was already running for the lift. He wasn't sure what he was going to do, just sure he had to do something. He frantically pressed the buttons, before giving up and running down the stairs, two at a time.

Liam left the ground through the iron gates and headed straight for the high street, guessing she was on her way to her flat. He could just make her out up ahead. Liam started to run.

"Wait!" he shouted, still running as fast as he could to catch her up before she got to the chemist. She heard him, but just quickened her pace. She didn't want him to see her like this. Tonight had been awful. She just wanted to get out of this town - away from Rangers, away from her dad, away from Liam, and to start again somewhere new.

Liam finally caught up with her by the alley at the side of the Royal Oak.

"Wait!" Liam said, grabbing her shoulder and spinning her around.

Bam! He received an almighty slap across the side of the jaw. He hadn't anticipated it, and it whipped his head to the side. Liam gathered himself and looked at Lisa. She was standing there glaring at him, her eyes ablaze, but all he could see were the tears streaming down her face. He had thought she didn't care, that she had been taking him for a ride. But as he saw her standing there fragile and vulnerable, he knew that wasn't true, and he felt foolish for his childish paranoia. He wished he had handled everything differently.

His eyes told her all this in a second and before he knew it Lisa had grabbed his head. Her hands were on either side of his face, then her lips were on his. He returned the kiss, pulling her closer to him, their pent-up emotion released in a moment of genuine, uncontrollable passion.

Eventually they pulled apart from each other.

"Lisa, I-"

He was interrupted by Lisa placing her finger on his lips. "It's ok Osborne. I know."

She took him by the hand in silence.

Later, lying on her bed, they talked long and deep, through the night and into the early morning, until the sunlight crept through her window. They spoke about their love for the club and the town, about her grandfather, about her father and his. They spoke about Billy and his problems settling into the footballing world. Explaining her reasons for secrecy, as well as why *her* and him could only have ever been friends. They spoke about her course and his career, and about her plans for the future. They also made promises to each other, and they swore with deep determination to keep them.

And, in the morning, he left.

Lisa lay alone. Her train was due to leave in just over an hour, but she tried to delay breaking the spell of the night before. She pondered the future. She knew that Liam would be a part of it - that she was sure of - but she was no clearer as to exactly what that future would look like. Her father was still her father, and she couldn't help but love him. But he was also Liam's boss, and as everyone had seen with Billy, it could be very dangerous for Liam if her father found out they were involved. Also, she was committed to her decision to move to Netfield, to make a better future for herself. But as she looked out of the window in the direction of Liam's estate, she felt a connection that she swore would not be broken.

Not by anyone.

Liam made his way home as the sun rose behind Clifton Park, home of Rangers. It was only as he was walking towards the estate, over the marshes and across the pitches where it all began, that he realised that they had made no plans to meet again in the near future. They hadn't even discussed a way of keeping in touch while she was away.

So the most incredible night of his young life ended, barely clearer than it had begun. Nonetheless, he knew in his heart that he had started on a path that he would not stray from, and this conviction consumed him. He was practically floating across the heath. Suddenly his walk turned into a hasty jog, as he realised that he had a lot of explaining to do when he got home!

Other books by Anthony Potts:

Follow Liam's journey in the next book in the series:
Star on the Rise

Paperback ISBN: 978-1-80369-431-3

Made in United States
Orlando, FL
04 November 2024

53451063R00117